THE MORBID MUSEUM

JAMES PACK

Cover photo by Mihail Marcri on Unsplash.

"The Demon's Favor" first published in Uncaged Book Reviews in October 2018.

"Where the Bullfrogs Gather" first published in Jitter Press in October 2018.

"Ceres" first published in The Bold Mom in October 2018.

Other Works by James Pack

Mushaburui: A Mental Health Journey (Nonfiction)
The Tommy Gun: A Novella

Black Chaos (Poetry)
Cats, Coffee, Catharsis (Poetry)
Men Are Garbage (Poetry)

To everyone still fighting their nightmares.
Don't stop fighting.

A Welcome Message

Welcome to the Morbid Museum, a place of horror, crime, suspense, and death. Death is the prevailing theme in everything one will find in the Morbid Museum. Be it death from war, murder, unexplained creatures, or the rising of the dead. Visitors will find it within the hallways of this gloomy gallery. One might fear they will find violence and gore, but this is not as extreme as might one expects. Some images and subjects are disturbing. We describe them as art more so than something gruesome. The Morbid Museum is a pillar of excellence in the presentation of death.

As curator and founder, I take great pride in this institution. Death has been a part of my family for generations reaching back to the dawn of time. One could call it the family business. Reapers and plague doctors fill my ancestral tree. This is where my vast knowledge of death has culminated. It is more than a passion or desire. It is a calling, a destiny, a birthright. It is not enough to say death fascinates me. Death is within me; within everyone. Some only choose not to see this. Some cannot accept death.

The Morbid Museum is unique. It encompasses all aspects of death, not only the horrific and fantastical. Death can be beautiful. Death can be simple. Death can be the mundane. There are plenty of killers, monsters, and madmen to go around. What of the ghosts? Those who have already died. Are they monsters? I propose they are more like the madmen. Death has many layers and to understand it, one must peel back every layer to see the whole. Some layers are ugly; some beautiful. Some layers are humorous and entertaining. Others leave one questioning everything they have learned.

The contributions from our patrons have helped the museum further expand its galleries. There is so much more to do. The mission of the Morbid Museum is to showcase death in all its forms, all its glory, and all its capacities. For those people afraid of dying or death, abandon all hope. A darkness looms over these exhibits and many may not find the strength to venture too far. There is no shame to anyone who chooses to turn back. We applaud them for knowing their capabilities.

Thank you to everyone who has graced our halls and to the future spectators and surveyors. The museum could not continue without the help of customers and supporters. These exhibits are informative, entertaining, and sinister in nature. Death is only the beginning. By facing the projects guests can face their own mortality and reconcile with that fear. I wish everyone a pleasant journey through our doors. I find no greater joy than seeing a satisfied customer. I only ask one favor of any who enter. Please visit the gift shop before leaving.

Siris Grim

Siris Grim

Curator/Founder
Morbid Museum, Inc

Contents

The Morbid Museum

Why Death Mister Grim?

There are many different perceptions of death. For some, it is something to fear and avoid; postponed for as long as possible. Some view it as a thing of beauty and a part of life. They wish to accept and embrace it. Some believe there is more to experience after death. Others believe death is the end and everything will be over. Debating these differences in belief would prove unproductive. There's no profit in it. The purpose of the Morbid Museum is to present death in all its forms. In all its horror. In all its beauty. All beliefs are welcome here.

This collection includes death in all its possible forms and versions. There are stories of humor, horror, valor, pain, and mystery. Death is open to such a broad interpretation; my museum is always growing. Some have asked why I have such a fascination with death. It, like an individual person and like life itself, is complex and comes in many forms. I encourage facing one's fears and the unknown. This can create immense trauma for some. For me (and others like me) this is nothing compared to the trauma I've already seen. Death has been the central theme of my life. My existence was born from others fears and misunderstanding of death. I have gone by many names and will have many more before my time has passed; before death has to die.

We have three primary exhibits; Trauma, Creatures, and the Supernatural. Each exhibit illustrates death in a different way. Every piece within the collections of each exhibit has a different story to tell. Some stories view death as the end while others view death as the beginning of a rebirth. Each morning we wake we are born again as each day is new, different, and full of possibilities. Some stories may appear out of place. Some spectators may feel exhibits did not include enough death. If one asks these questions, I hope they will look again with greater motivation. Death need not be the main focus for it to play a significant role in the story of a collection.

I am Siris Grim; Curator of the Morbid Museum and all things death. I am the Curate on this journey. I place the collections in order and choose which piece goes with each exhibit. I guide each visitor through the museum. Each tour holds stories for everyone of all ages. We recommend children enter with adult supervision. These stories are not for the faint of heart, but all are welcome in the Morbid Museum. Death awaits everyone. My museum offers viewers the opportunity to see Death in all its beauty and its ugliness. There is only one question a person needs to ask themselves before entering. Do you fear death?

Trauma Exhibit

Trauma is a distressing or disturbing experience. Sometimes trauma can cause a person to inflict trauma on others. Some will try to justify their actions as preventing future trauma. And sometimes trauma can keep one trapped in a nightmare forever. The pieces in this exhibit feature trauma from death. Characters are either surrounded by death or create death. Sometimes there's a little of both. Many of these pieces feel more believable in our own real world. Some do not, but trauma is universal as is death. Death captivates and traumatizes everyone in different ways.

The prevailing theme for this exhibit is the monstrous nature of humans. One may even call it the darkness within us all. Each piece features the worst humanity has to offer. Be it war, murder, or killing for sport and spectacle. Visitors will see primitive behaviors. The kind only thought of in nightmares. Some will ask how people do such things. Others will remember a time they saw something similar. Many will see a glimpse of themselves. The part they keep hidden or despise most. Trauma, like death, is not prejudice. All have the opportunity to experience the distressful and the disturbed.

Be warned, this exhibit is not for children or those weak at heart. Some of the depictions are gruesome or horrific. The kind of images that make many uncomfortable. There is no shame in choosing to skip this section of the museum. But, if one chooses to bypass one exhibit, they would do well to never enter the Morbid Museum. Proceed with caution through any exhibit. Death is never fun or merry. Death is solemn, beautiful, and mysterious. Trauma is never beautiful or solemn. Trauma breaks apart one's soul and hides the pieces. No one should wish trauma upon their worst enemy.

Jesse's Lament

During a quiet summer evening in Pennsylvania.
Only a few hours before a great battle would alter history;
this would become the bloodiest fight of the war. Upon a log
a few feet from camp, sat Jesse Wells. A young man from
Kentucky who had enlisted over two years ago when he was
17.

The war had only started. He had left behind his
family. A mother and father, two older sisters with children
of their own, and his twin brother, Wesley. He and Wesley
had argued many times before he left. Wesley didn't believe
in the North, he believed in the ideals of the South; of
People's and State's Rights. Jesse thought the South did not
want to give up slavery. Wesley, born two minutes before
Jesse, would claim to be smarter and older.

"You damned ignoramus! You think all this fightin'
is for them stupid niggers? I guess yer too young to
understand."

Wesley always scrutinized him because of the two-
minute difference. Two minutes did not seem like much to
Jesse, but it sure did to Wesley.

Wesley used to pick on Jesse for being smaller and
weaker. They were identical in every way; height, weight,
hair, eyes, they even had some of the same quirks. Would
they be the same now after two years of war? Jesse had
changed much from childhood. Now a man, fierce on the
battlefield and even more so in an argument. His heart had
calloused over into stone, Jesse grew cold.

In his first year of enlistment, he had seen small
children lying motionless on the ground. They were mistaken
for Confederate Soldiers and shot. Next to them, a dead

Union Soldier named Jones. When he realized they were children, he took his own life not able to live with the deed in his mind.

Everyone felt sympathy for him but Jesse thought, "The poor bastard! He couldn't handle the war." Some of the other men thought of Jesse as cold and black hearted having no feelings for anything.

Jesse agreed, at least, he wanted to be cold.

He would always say, "Emotions are useless; they get you killed in war!"

Everyone else would try to convince him the emotions made people human. Jesse felt humans were weak anyway.

As Jesse sat, a man with many stripes down the sleeve of his uniform approached from behind.

"How are you, Jesse?"

"I've been better Sergeant, you?"

"It's the same for me, Son. Our platoon will hold Culp's Hill tomorrow morning. As you know, your Squad Leader died earlier today at Cemetery Hill. Are you up to running the squad?"

"I suppose so. Until I'm dead or you find someone better."

The Sergeant reacted with a smile.

"We'll see you in the morning then."

As his superior left, Jesse thought how his brother would react. It is a leadership position; running a squad. Wesley would not find him so weak now. Haven't they grown older and wiser? Could Jesse and Wesley get along?

That night before retiring, Jesse wrote a letter home. He addressed it to Wesley, an apology letter of sorts. He thought after this battle he would be able to go home, even if the war continued. Though he lacked emotions, he did miss home and the relaxing time he would have there. He had no

10

time to reminisce of home life. He needed his rest for the morning. He felt the coming day would be hard and did not want to let his squad down.

The next morning was cool and humid. Everyone felt mentally prepared after having been through one day of fighting. Jesse's platoon took its position on Culp's Hill, ready to hold their ground. Should they fail, they would take as many "Reds" with them as possible.

In the distance, the Confederate flag waved through the air. Confederate soldiers followed. The words FORM A FIRING LINE!! echoed through the ranks as the Southern Soldiers began to charge. A few shots rang out and soon he heard the command to "fire at will."

Jesse needed time to reload and took cover behind a tree. Before he knew it, someone had spotted him and pinned him behind the tree. The confederate sat behind a large rock only a few feet from the tree. He reloaded his rifle. Jesse waited and placed a well-aimed shot towards his sniper. A direct hit to the head took the man down and some of Jesse's squad began to charge.

Jesse turned his opponent's body over and was not prepared for the sight. There lay his brother, Wesley; lifeless. He remembered all the fun they had as small boys, playing in wheat fields and creeks near their home. The companionship they had with each other and no one else, then he began to think of when they spoke last. He never apologized. He had not sent his letter off to home; it rested in his front jacket pocket. When did Wesley join the Confederate Army?

Jesse stood there stupefied in shock as a round lead ball raced through the air. It entered Jesse's eye, and ripped out the back of his head. Not more than two minutes after killing his brother, Jesse's life ended. After the horrible slaughter of the Battle of Gettysburg, someone discovered these two. Brothers who had died so close together, had both

11

written letters the night before to one another. Both dated July 1, 1863 and both apologizing to the lost brother. It seemed that despite their time apart, they were more in tune with one another than they were before. Two brothers born so close together, died by each other's side.

The Puppet Maker

I had a normal childhood. I grew up in a suburban home, always had presents for Christmas, with my best friend; my dog. My father made puppets. Every waking moment of the day he worked on his puppets or thought about new puppets. He made money as a carpenter. He made extravagant furniture and could create custom work on request. He enjoyed working with his hands. He felt he created real life.

My mother never liked his puppets hanging everywhere. He moved them to his workshop in the basement. She admired his craftsmanship, but he made so many. The final straw came when she found one in the bathroom. I had moved it there and forgot to put it back in the hall closet after I finished organizing and cleaning. My mother, furious, demanded all puppets get moved to the basement. I apologized to my father, but he didn't seem upset. He said he liked having all his creations in one place. He said it made him feel like God.

Everything changed when we heard about the puppet killer on the news.

They found puppets at the scene of the crime and these puppets looked like the victims. Police have not confirmed if the killer made the puppets.

The puppets on the TV looked different from the marionette puppets my father made. They looked almost alive. My father commented on the craftmanship but didn't say much else. My mother said nothing and continued reading her book. I'm not sure if she saw or listened.

The next day, the police arrested my father while he worked at his shop downtown. An anonymous tip told the police my father made puppets, so he immediately became a suspect. They searched our whole house and took all my father's puppets. My mother kept asking questions trying to understand the situation. All the officers said the same thing and told her to wait for the detective. We waited an hour before the detective came.

A short brunette woman dressed in a man's suit. I found it strange that a woman looked so nice and neat in a suit. She introduced herself as Detective Jiminy and apologized for not arriving sooner. My mother told me to go play in my room. I don't know how much time passed before my mother and the detective came to my room. My mother said the detective wanted to ask me some questions about my father.

Detective Jiminy asked if my father ever played with his puppets. I said he sometimes did, but he always told me he needed to test the strings. He wanted to make sure the arms and legs moved as designed. Then she asked if he ever made movies with the puppets. I said I didn't know. Then she asked if my father ever worked on his puppets somewhere else. Somewhere other than his shop in the basement or his shop at work. I said I didn't think so. Then she asked me if my father ever told me something and told me not to tell my mother. I said only when we bought her a birthday present last year. She asked if I remembered the present. I described the gold bracelet on my mother's wrist. The detective thanked me for my help and left the room with my mother. I couldn't hear what they said, but they kept talking.

When the detective and police left, I asked my mother when my father could come home. She said she didn't know but soon. I asked if the police thought my father made the puppets that killed people. She said she thought my father could help the police find the other man. She didn't want me to have negative thoughts toward my father.

Along with the puppet, the killer would also leave a video of puppets enacting the murder. It would always be in the same fashion the victim died. The police found the killer puppet and copies of the tapes in one of my father's marionettes. Someone bumped into a table, the puppet fell and broke. That's how they found the evidence to put my father away. If someone hadn't knocked over the puppets, they never would have found the evidence. It destroyed my mother. She learned about all these things my father hid from us. She couldn't take care of herself anymore and I didn't know how to take care of her. She overdosed on pills and died. I was nine. No one knew if she committed suicide or took too many pills.

My father wrote me a note before hanging himself in prison. He apologized for hurting me and my mother and for what happened to her. He asked me not to give up and to keep going. He told me he buried lots of money in our backyard and had lots of valuable things hidden in the house. He also had a bank account in my name. He called it my college fund. I never went to college. Years passed before I realized how much my parent's deaths affected me. The doctors said I didn't get upset when they died. It didn't bother me. I worried about my dog, they said, but no one knew where my dog went. I didn't tell them about the money. I didn't tell them I dug up the money. I didn't tell them I buried my dog in the same place as the money. I didn't tell them I killed my dog. I didn't tell them I liked watching him whine in pain as he died. But... I'm telling someone now. Well, I'm writing it in this journal, anyway. It's been fifteen years. I've killed many animals and many people since then. They called my father the Puppet Killer. What will they call me? I like to call myself Insanity.

Insanity Kills

Hello Detective,

I have the understanding you were the person who discovered my latest work. Believe it or not, of the many times I've killed, you are the first person that figured out my process. Kudos!

As you seem more gifted than so many others, I would like to tell you about my past projects. You may suspect I am some nut-job seeking attention, but you can verify my accounts with a little research. Also, I'm sure you have heard of my father. The media called him The Puppet Killer.

I'm telling you this because I'm upset with how efficient I've been at avoiding capture. What's the point of doing something if no one knows you did it? For this first of many letters, I would like to tell you how it all began for me; my first human kill. It all started in high school when I developed a crush on a lovely girl named Catherine.

Her sweet and kind words always lifted me from the darkness. She would call me wonderful and always wished me the best. One day I mustered up the courage to ask her out, to be more than friends. She denied my advance, claiming she already dated someone. Heartbroken and disappointed, I continued as I would each day. My father wanted me to keep going.

Sometime shortly thereafter, I went to see her at lunch as I always did. Before she noticed me, I overheard her telling her friends about the last time we spoke. She and her friends mocked me and called me names. I had heard many people call me names, but not her. I realized she meant none of the things she said. I couldn't let this betrayal go unpunished. There were many things I could have done to inflict as much pain on her as possible, but I had to be cautious and patient.

I needed to cause pain upon her with discretion. She could not know who caused it. She had to feel the emotional turmoil but also the confusion of not knowing why. This shielded me from retaliation.

The planning of my revenge consumed most my time. I had to study my prey without distraction. I acted as I always had to ensure no one would notice my true feelings. I learned all I could about everyone in her inner circle. I offered services, so they would accept me, and they were happy to have a servant of sorts. They assumed I wanted friendship and preyed on this. They were unaware of my true intentions.

I spent months gaining information on my enemies. I knew intricate details of their lives that even they were not aware. This gave me power. I positioned myself to manipulate their lives. I could do things to her friends, but they would not provoke an emotional response from her. Her friends had to get punished with her but how? This question plagued me for too long.

After some time, I planned to set fire to one of their homes. I hadn't decided whose home, but I thought this would be a good start for a series of events to invoke my revenge. Wait for everyone to leave the home and then set it ablaze. It had to look like an electrical fire, so no one would be suspect. I needed to do more research.

I spoke to my state appointed counselor. I've had one ever since I went into foster care after my parents' death. I told her of the betrayal and my wanting revenge but nothing else. She said these feelings are normal, but I shouldn't act on them.

A few days before I started the first part of my plan, things changed. We sat around one afternoon. I waited for someone to tell me to do something as I always did.

Catherine asked me for a favor. I obliged. Her boyfriend accused me of trying to steal his girl. I couldn't understand why he would be jealous of me. He shouted, and everyone tried to calm him down. In his rage, he punched me. I'd never felt so much physical pain before. Catherine yelled at him. She looked back at me and told me I should leave. I had never been so angry. My plans had to change. I disliked him before but now he needed severe punishment.

The thought of what to do came as though I always had the thought. I already had everything in place without realizing it. I waited for the right time. Everything had to be perfect. Several weeks had passed when the opportunity presented itself. Dickhead's parents went out of town one weekend. He held a party that Friday evening. With no invitation, I snuck in unnoticed. Most of the party happened downstairs or in the backyard. My plan would work best upstairs. One couple had taken over the master bedroom to relieve teenage sexual tension. Otherwise the second floor looked abandoned. I found his room and got to work. To make the fire look like an electrical short, I replaced one of the electrical plugs with a faulty one. I made sure I replaced a plug he didn't use and wouldn't notice. The flames would not start until tomorrow. I made my way back downstairs and out the door. No one even noticed me. The invisibility made me feel powerful.

I had to be patient in order for everything to work. Catherine and the douche bag had a date planned for the next night. I knew he would walk her home and then go back to his place; that's when I would strike. I waited behind some bushes as they made their way back to her house. He tried to persuade her into letting him come inside but her parents were home and wouldn't allow it. They kissed for a while before she finally went inside. He started back home, walking with his arrogant strut. I followed behind, closing the distance between us. He paid no attention. I walked behind him unnoticed. I readied the hatchet. I raised it in the air and with all my strength I struck him in the head. Blood splattered my mask, and I caught his body before it hit the ground.

I dragged him along the sidewalk with plastic around his head, so blood wouldn't drip everywhere. I struggled, but I got him up the stairs and into his bedroom. I lifted him on his bed and took the plastic off. I plugged his TV into the wall socket I had replaced the night before. It sparked at first but didn't catch fire. I grabbed the gasoline I had hidden in the garage and drenched the room and threw some on the TV cord. It sparked a fire, and I threw matches all over the room.

I had to make sure no one saw me leave. In silence, I went out the back and jumped the fence into another yard and then another fence. I made my way back to the street and back home. I could already see the flames rising from the window. I took pride in my achievement but had to move fast before someone noticed the fire. I made it all the way home before I heard any sirens. The fire had plenty of time to destroy any evidence. I slept like the dead that night.

The fire appeared on the news the next morning. Firefighters determined a faulty outlet caused the fire. No one suspected arson. Too easy. They showed Catherine on the news crying. I would have to wait awhile before I could finish my plan. It would be a few more years before my next kill. But you'll hear about that in my next letter, Detective.

With regards,
Insanity

Escape from Century

The cat gasped with heavy breathing as she woke. She felt something heavy on her arm. Like tentacles from the floor, chains enclosed around her wrists. She saw other animals around the room, unconscious and strapped to the floor. Their faces hidden in darkness. She thought some were dead. They occupied a small building with only two doors close to each other; with boarded windows. She feared sitting up. She did not want to draw attention to herself in case the Humans were watching. She heard a deep, unfamiliar voice from behind her.

"What's your name?"

She rolled over and saw another cat off in the corner with his face hidden in shadow. The stranger sat upright unlike the others. In this position, he seemed to tower over them, giving off a commanding presence.

"What's your name? Do you speak English?"

"Yes! Reid. My name is Reid. Who are you?"

"Anthony."

"How long have you been here?"

"A day or two." Anthony said.

"Any idea what happens here?"

"No. Some have guessed interrogation, others medical experiments. I can't say for sure."

Something flew over the building. The roar of its engine vibrated the entire structure.

"SADD's have been making rounds every ten minutes. I guess they're expecting us to escape." Anthony said.

"SADD's? You mean the planes?"

"It means Search and Destroy Drones. That's what I call their planes. They're flown by remote. Can I ask what you were dreaming?"

Reid hesitated. She looked around then sat up to Anthony's level.

"My brother and I were searching for food. We looked everywhere, old ruins, abandoned homes, any place we thought we could find food. Even places we didn't. Then the Humans came. All we had to defend ourselves were shotguns but few shells. One of them got a hold of Jesse, my brother, snapped his neck and threw him back towards me. I lost all rational thought and unloaded everything I had on them. When I ran out of ammo, I tried beating them with the butt of the weapon. The Humans backed off. I saw a figure coming toward me. I couldn't make it out at first. I saw my little sister. I knew it had to be a trick because she died when the bombs hit. But what if she was real? That's when she grabbed me. As she strangled me, her eyes turned white. Then I woke up here. How could I have remembered what she looked like? I haven't seen her in years. I do not even have a picture, not of anyone."

"I only have one picture of my mother. Someone took it a few months before I was born."

He pulled something from his jacket pocket and handed an old, dirty photo to Reid. She examined it. It felt like a thin, brittle piece of paper and had a corner missing. Reid speculated the photo was at least twenty years old. The Cat in the picture looked young, younger than Reid, and had a sad, cold look on her face.

Reid examined the photo for a long time. It mesmerized her.

"She's pretty. What was her name?"

"Sarah. She died a few years before the invasion; before the bombs hit. The day Humans tried to exterminate the animal race. The day the Humans declared war on us."

Anthony said this to himself more than answering Reid's question. Neither spoke for a while. Reid returned the picture.

"This picture gave me good luck in the past but..."

Anthony trailed off examining the bar code burned onto his right forearm.

"... it doesn't seem to work anymore."

Another SADD flew overhead, and they heard explosions in the distance. Anthony looked at Reid.

"You should sleep. You'll need all your strength tomorrow." He said.

"What happens tomorrow?"

"This is a work camp. If they think you can't work, they kill you."

"I thought you didn't know what went on here." Reid said.

"I don't know what they do at night, but during the day, they use the animals as slave labor. Cleaning up the bodies from the most recent raids. From the number of explosions, I'd say we've got lots to clean up tomorrow."

Reid found sleeping difficult with explosions and the blood-curdling screams from outside. Everything quieted, and Reid dozed into a light sleep. Nothing compared to the nightmares she dreamt. She saw her dead sister again with white eyes.

Despite the nightmares, Reid felt rested. She woke to the sound of creaking floors and clanking of chains. One Human gathered everyone and led them outside. She noticed fewer people than the night before. Even Anthony, her new friend, disappeared.

The Human picked up an old dog close to Reid. The old dog lifted his left arm for the Human to release his restraint, stood up and waited for new wristbands. He acted accustomed to this routine.

The Human approached Reid. She thought it best not to resist. The sun blinded her; it sat low in the sky. Piles of rubble, garbage and scraps of steel rested all around her prison. The Humans had reinforced the building with sheet metal siding covering steel beams. She walked behind the old dog with her chains latched to his. Each animal bore shackles around their ankles linked to each prisoner.

With the last animal connected; the Humans signaled for the first one in line to walk. Everyone followed.

"Where are they taking us?"

"It's best not to talk now. Wait till we get to the work site." The old dog said.

Reid understood when she saw a Human stop and watch everyone as they passed. They kept a close eye on everyone as they marched. All she knew; they marched to a work site.

The militant march felt like hours though the sun was low in the sky. They passed a cleared area about the size of a baseball field. Many animals gathered corpses and threw them in the back of vehicles. Only a few Humans surrounded the perimeter with little rods sticking out of the ground in front.

Reid recognized one animal working. Anthony looked up and nodded his head towards her. Reid returned the gesture.

A small frail monkey ran away from the shuffling slaves towards an open area between two Humans. Neither moved to intercept her. Two jolts of electricity shot from the rods on either side of her. Fifty yards away; Reid smelled the burnt hair and flesh as the smoking body hit the ground. Some animals in line ahead of her stopped in shock. Others in the chain gang pushed and pulled to keep everyone moving. One Human threw the monkey onto the pile of bodies; burnt, lifeless and smoldering.

23

The sun rose out of their eyes when they arrived at their destination. They trudged into the center of the area and the Humans placed rods around the group. A continuous circle of electricity surrounded them for a moment then dissipated. The Humans removed restraints. Those familiar with their duties carried and dragged bodies to the waste trucks. The Humans passed unaffected by the voltage. Once they were out of the contained area, animals explained duties to the newcomers.

Reid went to the dog she spoke to before.

"What do they do with the bodies?"

"No one knows." The dog said.

"How long have you been here?"

"A year. I'm not sure. It's pointless to keep track of time anymore."

"How often do we work?"

"Depends on how close the battle is to our camp. Sometimes it's several weeks before they let us out of the bunker. What's your name?"

"Reid."

"Sergeant Perry. I guess that title means nothing now. You got any family?"

"I have a brother. I've lost everyone else."

"That's a shame. I was lucky. Most of my family made it. We decided on a last-minute camping trip when the attack happened. We were all in the middle of nowhere. The closest nuke was about ten miles from us, so we had plenty of warning. Before they captured me, I had the largest surviving family anyone knew. They all could be dead by now though..."

"So, do you have any idea where we are?"

"If I remember my geography, we're somewhere around what used to be Palomas."

"Isn't there a river near here? It wouldn't be difficult to escape to…"

"Listen Reid and listen well. There's no chance of escape. Many have tried, and they all failed, you saw that monkey back there. Get the thought out of your head now and you'll live longer!"

Perry walked away. More and more questions filled Reid's mind. She wondered what Anthony thought. With a sigh, she gritted her teeth and grabbed another body.

The day dragged forward. The Humans brought out a water jug and gave the workers breaks. The water felt cool and refreshing.

A bear noticed the contorted expression on Reid's face.

"Giving us water helps us be more efficient." The bear said.

As the sun fell, the last bodies filled the trucks. The Humans lined everyone up and connected them with the iron ropes. With the animals secured, they removed the electric rods. They passed the site where the monkey died. The clearing sat empty and lifeless. They returned to the makeshift prison by dark and the Humans escorted them inside one by one. Anthony and the others waited for them, and though she wanted to speak with him again, Reid wished for sleep. As soon as they latched her to the floor, Reid fell into a deep sleep.

"Hey, I got you!" A young kitten said.

"No, you didn't!" Another kitten said.

"Yes, I did! I got you Jesse! You never play fair!"

"Shut up, Reid! You're jealous cause I'm older than you!" Jesse said.

"Well, I'm smarter than you!"

"No, you're not!"

"Yes, I am!"

25

"Will you two stop fighting? That's all you do, you're supposed to be brother and sister, but you never get along!" Their mother said.

"She started it!" Jesse said.

"No, I didn't, you did!"

"Knock it off you two or you're both grounded. Now get inside and wash up; it's time for dinner."

"Yes, Mom."

They lowered their heads and shuffled inside. Not realizing their mother could see them, Reid and Jesse stuck their tongues out at each other.

"Knock it off before I cut your tongues out!"

While at the dinner table, the two kittens gave each other dirty looks. Their younger sister giggled.

Their mother collected plates from the table. A large man with white eyes forced his way through the back door. He pulled out a 9mm handgun and executed the family. Reid ran into the living room as Jesse hid under the table. Reid saw the man kill her family, throw the table to the side and point his gun at Jesse. Reid tried to run and stop him but the more she ran the farther away she moved from the dining room. She watched in slow motion, the man pulled the trigger and sent the bullet twirling in the air towards Jesse's head. Reid screamed an inaudible scream. As the bullet hit him, Jesse's head jerked back. A splatter of blood and brains covered the wall behind him. Everything became black and white except the blood on the wall. The man turned towards Reid. Out of fear, she could not move. The man pointed his pistol at Reid...

"NOOOO!"

Reid screamed as she jerked into the air only to get yanked back down by the chain latched to her wrists. She held her side in pain as she looked at all the faces staring at her. Her screams woke up many animals. No one said a word. She rolled over to go back to sleep and saw Anthony sitting in his corner; unaffected by the screams. Reid continued to stare at Anthony until his image disappeared into darkness.

A road in the desert appeared from the darkness. Reid walked along and saw a gas station come into view. When she arrived, everyone was motionless. A rabbit stood near the gas pump, a young bunny running inside the building, and a cat sat in a car. She faced forward with no movement. Reid looked the same direction the cat looked. At first, she saw nothing, then she saw a bright flash. Once her eyes readjusted, she saw a huge cloud building from far off. It shaped itself like a giant mushroom. Then a wall of fire came roaring over the mountain. Reid ran but saw no one else moving.

"HEY!"

No one acknowledged. She went to the cat and tried to shake her, but she sat frozen and did not budge. The firry wall closed on her. Reid gave up on the cat and ran. She could not run fast enough. The fire caught up. She felt the heat on her back as she turned...

Reid woke but instead of screaming, she coughed and gagged. Now morning, the same people watched her, as if they never stopped.

"Rough night?" Perry said.

"Something like that."

"No work today! Try to catch up on your sleep."

Reid nodded and laid back down on the hard, uncomfortable wooden floor.

The sun rose over a snow-covered mountain. The smell of the rain lingered in the air from the night before. The hard rain made the ground moist. A log cabin sat in a small clearing of trees. A bearded goat stepped onto the porch. He collected firewood and placed them inside. He returned with

27

his rifle over his shoulder. He stepped off towards the forest. The man stopped. He looked alarmed.

"REID?" he said.

How does he know my name?

"REID?"

His deep voice echoed across the forest.

"What do you want?"

"REID?"

"Who are you?"

The man loaded his rifle. He aimed forward and before he pulled the trigger…

"WAKE UP, REID!" Perry said.

"Wha? Whatsit?"

"They're moving us. They move camp every few weeks. You need to wake up!"

Perry had a hint of fear in his words.

A Human busted the door open startling everyone. They were violent as they gathered prisoners. One fox tried to resist, and the Human threw him through a wall; his arm still hooked to the chain connected to the floor. It twitched about looking for its body, squirting blood. No one had the urge to resist anymore. They ripped the chains from the floor and dragged animals four at a time.

Nails stuck out of the floor. Reid felt each one as they ripped her clothes and cut her back. The sun sat high in the sky and blinded Reid as she laid on her back. The air felt warm and full of dust. Most of the dirt caught on her sweaty face and arms. The Humans pulled her to her feet and threw her behind the line of chained animals. Reid saw Anthony get pulled out shortly after her. He looked tougher than Reid. She saw Perry a few animals ahead of her. Her only two friends at least were still alive. Reid wondered if she could talk on this journey. Reid nudged the raccoon in front of her.

"Where are they taking us this time?"

28

"I'll tell ya when I find out!"

"Well, what's your name then?"

"Number 235419365 according to the Humans."

Light chatter rose from the line of animals. The Humans did not mind as long as everyone kept moving.

"So, are you going to tell me your real name or do you want me to call you 235419365?"

"Jamie!"

"Reid."

"You got any more questions, Reid?"

"How long have you been here?"

Jamie sighed.

"We were only there for about three weeks. They usually move us every month. I've been here six moves. Jones and Scarborough came in with me. We're the only ones still alive from that bunch. Perry's been here the longest. Most of the animals that came in your group won't live to the end of the week; you may not live either."

"How d'you manage it?"

"We don't resist. We do what they tell us, and we stay alive. Most animals don't take well to captivity."

Reid had plenty of time to get to know her new comrades. The obvious idea for staying alive did not involve fighting. Reid felt fighting would be the only way to stay alive. They walked past dusk. The moon floated part of the way in the sky. The Humans stopped to let everyone rest for the night.

They set up their electric perimeter. Once everyone settled themselves, many laid about stargazing. Reid could not remember the last time she saw something so beautiful. Before her capture, Reid would sneak out with her brother and they would watch the stars. Those not admiring the sky fell asleep. Anthony did neither. He sat up watching the Humans. Reid sat with him.

29

"How are you, Anthony?"

"Still alive, same as you."

"You've been watching them for a while."

"I'm learning how they operate. How they react to their surroundings. I'm trying to understand them."

"You're not planning on escaping, are you?"

"Well, that wouldn't be wise, would it?"

Reid wondered what Anthony thought.

"I know your brother. Jesse. I found him several months ago. He fought every Human he could searching for you. I asked him to join my group. He wouldn't come with us unless we agreed to help search for you. They put you in this camp a few days ago. Where've you been?"

"I'm happy he's alive. I've gone through many camps. I always escaped, but it didn't take long for them to catch me again. Each camp had higher security than the last. I've heard the highest security was at Century Work Camp, but it's only rumored."

"Well kid, you're in Century."

The statement echoed through Reid's mind. She considered it once before but put it away. Escape did not seem possible here.

Reid did not feel like talking anymore. She reclaimed her section of dirt and tried to sleep. She feared closing her eyes. The thought of more nightmares plagued her. She gazed up at the moonlit sky; a beautiful sight with no clouds in the star-speckled night. Finally, the young cat's eyes became too heavy. The beauty of the night faded to darkness.

"Why did you leave me?"

A young cat stared off as a human stood behind him with a weapon pointed at his head.

"You left me to die." The young cat said.

The human squeezed the trigger, and the cat fell forward. The cat lay there with lifeless eyes, but his mouth kept moving, repeating its words.

"Why did you leave me? Why did you leave me? Why did you leave me?"

Reid's body shot up as the horn blew. The Humans woke all the animals to continue moving. Reid looked around for those she knew as the Humans returned the animals to shackles. Before she could see any of them, a Human pushed her back to chain her to a rabbit. The rabbit came in with Reid's group. The rabbit's ears rested behind her head, but she shook and glanced at everything moving. Her eyes, restless and fidgeting.

"We'll be all right. They're moving us again." Reid said.

"I know. That doesn't make me less nervous. I've never gotten captured before." The rabbit said.

"We'll get out of this. I've broken out of lots of prisons and camps. The Humans can never hold me for long."

"Forgive me if I'm not as confident as you are."

"What's your name?"

"Angel. They brought you here the same day as me, right?"

"Yeah, I'm new here too. My name's Reid. Follow everyone else's lead and the Humans won't pay much attention to you. It's the best way to survive for now."

"I'm not the resisting type. I've seen too many of my friends die. I never fought the Humans. They took my family's farm and captured those of us who didn't fight. The ones that did, they killed. My whole family's gone."

"I'm sorry. We better stay quiet for now until we stop moving."

31

They walked the full length of the day, watching the sun glide across the sky. As the sun fell and twilight began, they arrived at a series of brick buildings in ruin. The Humans restrained them into the largest of the buildings. Shackles lay dispersed along the concrete floor and brick walls. This building held more animals than the previous one. Reid saw everyone including Anthony, Perry, Jamie, and her newest friend Angel. Everyone waited for the Humans to leave in silence.

"This is the place." Anthony said.

He stood, chained to the wall, on the other side of the room opposite Reid.

"I know that look, Son. Whatever you're thinking, get rid of the idea now." Perry said.

"Have you ever been in a place with so many buildings since you came to this camp?"

"We're usually in make shift tin shacks the Humans put together after they destroy a city."

"Exactly. There've never been many places to hide when escaping. Now there are. We'll be out of the range of their weapons before they notice we've gone. If we can get to the wood line in time, the SADDs can't track each of us."

"Let's say we all get out of our chains. Let's say we get out of the building unseen and past all the buildings unseen. Let's say we make it to the woods either unseen or before the drones can reach us. Let's say we're able to keep out running the Humans until we lose them. Where do we go?"

"We find her brother Jesse."

"Why my brother?"

"He leads the resistance against the Humans. He started after he refused to join my group."

"What? Scrawny little Jesse? You're joking."

"When's the last time you saw him?"

32

"A couple years, I guess."

"Exactly. He's changed a lot. And you are nothing like the stories he told me so I'm sure you've changed a lot too."

"I never thought about it that way."

"What's your plan then, Hot Shot? Where do we find her brother?" Perry said.

"I don't know where he is. I thought she might know. I'm surprised the Humans don't know who she is." Anthony said.

"Isn't there a way to contact the resistance?" Reid said.

"The only way I know is to find my contact. He's in the northern territory. We still have to escape."

"Well, let's focus on one problem at a time. First, we have to get unshackled." Perry said.

"I can pick locks. I don't know how to leave without anyone noticing. I need time to get a layout of this place." Reid said.

"No problem there. I've been here before." Anthony said.

"How convenient!" Perry said.

"Is there a problem, Sergeant?"

"You know a lot about the Humans and the places they go. I've always been the suspicious type."

"Know your enemy, Sergeant."

"It'll take more than that for me to trust you."

"Then trust me. I know I can get us out of here. I've escaped every other camp the Humans have. They haven't built a cage that can hold me yet." Reid said.

"Do you trust him?" Perry said.

"Only enough to get out of here but I have little trust beyond that."

Everyone nodded in agreement. Anthony described an escape route to the forest. They considered disarming a few guards and taking their weapons. Reid felt confident they could get all the animals out.

Anthony lined out the plan. It would be easy to take down the few guards and run for the forest. If they made it before the next drone flyby, it would be hours before anyone noticed they left. No one had a way of keeping time.

After a long day's work, everyone slept for a couple hours. Reid had to free herself from the chains and wake everyone when the time came. Her nightmares and the anxiety of the escape prevented her from sleeping. She waited.

The night echoed with noise and movement. A drone interrupted every few minutes of peace. Snoring and stirring occupied the silence between flights. Along with laughter and talking from Human guards walking around the camp. Reid never heard them speak before and definitely never heard them laugh. She listened to every sound waiting for the time to wake everyone. She kept track of time by counting the number of passes by the drones. She estimated two-and-a-half hours had passed.

She unlocked her chains when she decided not to sleep. She woke and freed Anthony first, then Perry. They woke everyone else as Reid removed chains. They waited for the next drone. As it flew by, they told everyone to get ready and be alert. They would run after the next drone passed.

Alert and silent, no one moved. They heard no guards walking around. All the animals looked up; listening, waiting. Reid saw the plan unravel in her mind as one giant failure. She could see everything going wrong. As she envisioned everyone's death, a faint roar in the distance captured her attention.

34

The moment they waited for came. The drone passed overhead like before and Anthony took the lead. He pulled the door open and discovered the chain around the handles. He pulled Reid forward. She popped the lock open. Two guards walked by. They waited for the guards to pass before walking out. Anthony led them around the building. Everyone remained quiet except for their feet on the dirt. Before they would run to cover, Anthony checked that no Humans stood nearby. They got to the last building, and they heard the roar of the approaching drone.

"We're all not going to make it." Anthony said.

"We'll wait for the drone to pass." Reid said.

Humans shouted a few buildings away.

"No time! We've got to move now!" Anthony said.

Everyone raced for the tree line. The drone spotted them and fired on the stragglers. Reid turned to see her newest friend, Angel, the rabbit, bombarded by bullets. The scene looked like one of her nightmares. Fighting against her emotions, Reid kept running. She only saw Anthony ahead of her. Many were behind her, but everyone disappeared in the forest. They had no time to look for each other or regroup. The Humans searched the tree line.

Reid followed Anthony; she didn't want to be alone. This gave her something to focus on so she didn't think about Angel's death. Others died, but she didn't know them. She didn't know Angel either but something about watching her die felt too familiar. Had she dreamt it before?

Reid and Anthony stopped to catch their breath. They could not stay for long. They waited and listened. They heard screams and gunfire from far off. The Humans caught or killed someone. They moved away from the sound. The forest became more dense making running dangerous. They climbed over dead tree trunks and avoided roots growing out of the ground. The sounds of Humans and assault rifles faded away. They kept walking despite their exhaustion until sunrise.

Reid dropped herself to the ground. She removed her shoes and socks. She messaged her feet and rubbed cold dirt on them.

"We should keep moving." Anthony said.

"You should shut up. We need rest."

"The Humans could be right behind us."

"And they would have caught up to us a long time ago. We can relax for ten minutes. I've escaped a lot of places; trust me, we're okay for now."

"Well, excuse me for being more concerned about staying alive."

"You're concerned about keeping yourself alive. You didn't seem too worried about everyone else when they got shot down."

"We can't always save everyone. I assumed you already knew that."

"That doesn't mean you shouldn't try. We could have fought off the Humans until the drone passed."

"And they could have killed us or signaled the drone."

"But did we have to wait behind each building? We could have moved faster."

"And the Humans would have noticed our escape sooner and they would have called the drone back sooner. It would have gone bad no matter what. The important thing is that we survived."

"Do you even know any of their names? Did you talk with anyone besides me? Do you care that they've died?"

After saying this, Reid's ears rang. She saw Anthony speaking but there were no sounds. She saw the world turn sideways and everything faded to black. She didn't feel the fall or the foam coming from her mouth.

"What the hell happened?"

A Human stood in front of several hospital beds wearing a long white lab coat. Another Human in a lab coat with two nurses stood next to him.

"She seized but we've stabilized her."

"What was the cause?"

"Her mind is resisting. She's not allowing us to access her long-term memory."

"Dammit, Anthony, you said you could get the location of the rebel animals from this cat."

"I don't think she knows. She and her brother Jesse haven't seen each other in several years since the war began. I doubt she knows any rebels."

"She's still a priority prisoner. She's escaped too many of our facilities."

"What should we do with her?"

"Give her a new scenario. We know little about the leader of the rebellion; her brother. Her memories may give us the information we need to fight him. If you can get it done, I'll see that you receive a permanent position here at the Century Medical Facility."

"Yes, Sir. I'll make sure I'm with her the entire time to avoid further complications."

"You weren't with her the whole time before?"

"No, Sir. I thought I would gain more trust if I acted as a mysterious figure. Someone more reserved. Someone she could relate to. I suspect that's why the program failed."

"Do whatever you have to. I need that information if we want to end this war. These animals need to learn their place."

Gladiators

     The Arena (narrator) – They conceived and built me for a purpose; to present and entertain. People come from far away to enter my walls and partake in the slaughter. They call me the Arena or the New Coliseum. These titles mean nothing to me. It is what they wish to call me; they who control the weak and own the passive. I dream of freedom but mine is a life of servitude. Even if the killing stopped with me left alone, I would wither away without maintenance. I am a creature that cannot survive without my builders. And I have no choice in my purpose. Domination is to live, and freedom is to die. I must endure out of fear of destruction.

     For many years, the battles have taken place inside me. My walls built with sweat and blood only to have more blood creep across my sandy belly. I have seen so much death and it disgusts me. Yet the spectators, my builders, the people within my walls cherish these moments. How could anyone stand these cold walls stained with crimson? How can all those people bring their families within me to cheer the pain and suffering of others? My builders, these humans; they are a savage race. They build such spectacular structures to house the most appalling atrocities in nature. And I can only watch. I am the spectator who houses the spectators.

     I cannot speak of what happened before my construction. They completed my body in 2084. They spent years and unthinkable amounts of money developing me. The first battle under my skin was so gruesome. Prisons were overflowing so they reinvented the criminal rehabilitation program. They decided to have most of the criminals kill each other. They decided if someone survived ten battles, they were free but exiled. No one has ever survived more than five in the last fifteen years. Where was a winner of ten battles exiled? They decided to make that choice when they had a winner. As the years progressed, they began seeking gladiators from other places. There are not only criminals roaming the lower halls of my body. Political activists and rebels come through in droves. Anyone who fights or speaks out against them they condemn to death on my battlefield. If they could hear my words, they would sanction my destruction like the fighters. I can do nothing but watch their demise and lament. Now it's time for their puppets to take the stage and guide the spectacle.

GLADIATOR BOWL XV PREGAME SHOW

Bret – It's January 31, 2099 and we are ready to get our pregame show underway. Welcome to Gladiator Bowl 15! We're broadcasting into the ether from the lunar surface. Hello, I'm Bret Stevens.

Sue – And I'm Sue Ellen White. Thank you for tuning in on this beautiful Sunday afternoon. We have some pretty awesome battles coming up within the next hour.

Bret – That's right Sue; it'll be quite the gore fest this year. Let's review some of our contenders we're going to see today. As always, our first battle will consist of about two hundred or so nameless criminals. These are our first timers in the New Coliseum, and we throw them into a free-for-all battle. Everyone is against each other. Anyone left standing after the fifteen-minute battle will fight in level two next year.

Sue – Few remain after one of these fights, but survivors will be one step closer to earning their freedom.

But those that survive today will still have nine more battles before they can go home.

Bret – It is gruesome. Parliament approved criminal fighting 16 years ago. Since then, the crime rate has dropped 83 percent. It has made the planet safer and provided a great deal of entertainment for everyone. What's the next battle we have in store for our viral crowd Sue?

Sue – Well Bret, the next fight is level two. Our lucky survivors from the bloodbath last year. They return as well-trained fighters ready to take on greater challenges. The gridiron fills with two teams of 25 fighters each. Whichever team gets the other team's flag in the allotted time wins the match. If no team has the other's flag before time runs out, then whichever team has the most fighters still alive wins. The losing team is immediately executed.

Bret – I guess you could call it Survivor the Real Game.

Sue – Ha! I suppose you could Bret.

Bret – And be sure to watch the Season Finale of Survivor: Mars, this Tuesday here on UBC. What else is in store for our viewers this fine Sunday afternoon, Sue?

Sue – Rounding out the first half, the third battle pits two teams of five against each other. They fight for the honor of upgrading from nameless fighters to mighty warriors. Whichever team survives wins the honor. Never have we seen all team members survive one of these battles. The most on record is two team members surviving, is that right Bret?

Bret – It sure is Sue. Usually only one survives one of these matches and only once were there no survivors. That was back in 2091, Gladiator Bowl VII. The officials had a big chore trying to figure out what to do for the half time Naming Ceremony. Fans raved about it for months.

Sue – Well let's hope we get to see a naming ceremony today, Brett. And after the ceremony, at the top of the second half, we have our first major battle. Some of our new and upgraded fighters will do battle until only one fighter remains. There's no time limit for this fight. It starts with two teams of two. If both members of one team survive, they must fight each other until one survivor of the four walks free.

Bret – For this match we have Athena and Andromeda fighting against Artemis and Apollo. This will be the match of the decade with Artemis and Apollo who are brother and sister. They may have to fight each other by the end of the match. They were the fan favorite last year and most of the crowd is here to see this fight.

Sue – You know, Bret, it seems like most of the crowd is here for the final battle between Prometheus and Talos.

Bret – You might be right. This is a serious day for our current champion Prometheus. If he wins today, he will hold the record for the most victories in the final round with six. He currently has five. After ten victories, fighters retire and earn their freedom from captivity. Talos is hoping to earn his first victory if he can defeat Prometheus. The stakes are high for both these fighters. To add to the excitement, we

41

release tigers and lions onto the battlefield. Rumor has it they're extra hungry this year.

Sue – Everyone loves those lions. Let's check in with our field correspondent Don Michaels and see how things are on the sidelines. Don?

Don – Sue. Bret. Thank you. I'm so glad to be here for Gladiator Bowl 15. I'm looking forward to the carnage.

Bret – Do we have any fun pregame stuff going on down there right now?

Don – We sure do, Bret. The Glamiators are getting ready to take the arena. This is a special occasion and a sad occasion for the Glamiators as one of their members is retiring. Terence Broadchurch has been with the Glamiators since the first Gladiator Bowl. He was 17 years old making him the youngest person on the team. Several men, women, other genders, and aliens joined and left the team over the years. He is stepping down from performing but will continue as a coach and trainer.

Sue – Do you think you could catch him after their performance, Don? Can you find out why he chose to coach?

Don – Sure thing, Sue. In the meantime, I can tell you about how the Glamiators got started along with the Gladiator Bowl. The first Gladiator Bowl wasn't actually televised across the net. It was a live event full of death and mayhem. Each fighter in that first year fought in several battles and only a few survived. The first naming ceremony wouldn't take place until the next year. This is also when the Glamiators made their first appearance along with Terence.

That original group only lasted two years. You may recall the tragic accident in year four. One of the fighters during the final battle overthrew his weapon. The weapon killed everyone's favorite Glamiator Rebecca the Glamazonian Bombshell. To this day fans continue to mourn her passing. Many are holding her photos in the stands today. Fun Fact! That fighter who took Rebecca from us. He was one of the first fighters to receive a name at the first naming ceremony. He was also the first to win four consecutive final battles.

Bret – Isn't there a lot of controversy over how many battles he won?

Don – That's right, Bret. Kronos was one of the survivors from the first year which they included in his total wins. He went undefeated until year five when, like the Ancient Greek Myth, he died by the hand of Zeus. Zeus would go on to win five battles before losing to our current champion Prometheus.

Sue – Thanks for the quick history lesson, Don. We'd like to give a quick shout out to our sponsors. Halifax Foods and Beverage, Space 9, and our main sponsor for the last 15 years Moon Dust Lite. The lager with the smooth crisp taste.

The Arena – They laugh at the fallen and departed. They crave only money and blood. The crowds don't even have respect for my walls and floors. They leave trash and filth all over. Some can't even restrain themselves and wait for the bathroom. There are signs marked and bathrooms placed near every exit. Still they relieve themselves in the nearest corner. Human beings are filthy creatures. It's remarkable how the species has survived so long. Thousands of years of evolution. All they can do is intoxicate themselves, fornicate, and kill each other. Any other species would be extinct. How have they survived? They may even outlive me. If I am destroyed, I hope it is to end the horror that they create inside me. I didn't ask for this. They forced it upon me. I am helpless. I'll never get rid of these vermin.

Bret – Let's move down to the field for the corporate anthem.

Unknown Voice – Get down on the ground, now!

Other Voice – It's time for this carnage to end!

Bret – There's something happening outside the control booth.

Sue – Oh My God!

Don – Sue? Brent? Is everything okay up there?

EXPLOSION

Don – Oh my God! There's been an explosion in the control booth. Debris is falling into the crowd. There's been another explosion by the gate where fighters enter the field. People are being trampled trying to escape. The dome around the arena is cracking. We need to go now! Forget the camera, there's no time!

EXPLOSION

Voice Over – We are the People's Front of Serenity. This place has committed crimes against humanity for too long. We judge and sentence you to death. This will be the last day of carnage. May God have mercy on you all.

The Arena – I hear screams. I smell my burning structure. How strange humans are. They fight death and carnage with more death and carnage. What is this People's Front that is destroying me? I have no complaints. I'm happy to go if it means no more death within me. But why cause greater death with my death? These foolish mortals. Their lives are brief, and they never understand how to create things that thrive and grow. They can only destroy and create things that make them better destructors. How have they lived so long? The dome above me will break soon and all will be silent. And yet, there are still humans holding cameras. They watch the death and mayhem ignoring their imminent demise. Do they only care about destroying themselves? The dome breaks. Silence at last. And peace.

The Ghosts Inside

Flashing lights illuminated the small wooded area as twilight transitioned into dawn. Three police patrol cars waited for a fourth sedan. As the driver of the sedan got out of his vehicle, the other police officers followed. Together, they walked over to a nearby river to examine the nude body of a small boy floating in the water.

The oldest of the three police officers looked at the man from the sedan.

"She found him about an hour ago."

He pointed to the woman sitting in the back of his squad car.

"What was she doing here?" The man from the sedan said.

"Jogging!" The officer said. "We're still waiting for the ME; he should be here in about 15 minutes."

The man from the sedan said nothing.

"Would you like us to search the area detective?" The officer said.

The detective walked back to his car.

"The body floated downstream; this isn't the dump site. I wouldn't spend too much time here."

The detective returned to his sedan and made a phone call.

The youngest of the three officers asked, "How the Hell does he know?"

"That's Detective Riggins." The older officer said. "He's seen every kind of murder there is; he can see things no one else does."

"This is Sergeant Ledesma."

An accented female voice resonated through the detective's cell phone.

"Viviana, it's Ted. I need you to look up an old case file from about five years ago. It was a murder investigation of a young boy; a cold case."

"Do you think it has something to do with this new body?"

"Would I have asked for it if I didn't?"

The annoyance in Ted's voice made him sound even more sarcastic than he intended.

"Can't you answer me like a mature adult for a change?"

"I will when you stop asking me stupid questions. I'll be at the department in an hour after I get breakfast."

Ted ended the call and threw his phone in the passenger seat. He had known Viviana for several years. They had never worked together until recently when she got promoted and placed in charge of his unit. Only a year after their affair which led to Viviana's divorce. They had spoken little since.

"Did you get that case file I asked for?" Ted strutted past Viviana as he handed her one coffee he was carrying.

"It's on your desk. Does this have two creams and no sugar?"

"The way you like it."

Getting her coffee was the closest Ted would get to apologizing. He never spoke an apology in his life and always made a gesture instead. It was frustrating but Viviana recognized it as a piece offering. Ted picked up a compact disc on his desk. He didn't see a folder.

"Is this the case file?"

"Yeah, archives transferred everything to digital. It's supposed to be on an online database, but the IT guys are still working out issues, so they sent us that."

47

Ted was a little reluctant in accepting the new changes to his investigative process. He preferred looking at the actual file.

Despite his misgivings, he put the disc in his computer and reviewed the files. Someone threw everything on the disc; no organization. It would take a lot of time to go through all these computer files. Ted was still awaiting the autopsy reports which wouldn't be complete for a couple more hours. Sitting at his desk for even a half hour was not the most desirable activity on a Saturday morning.

After about an hour, Ted had finally found and reviewed all the crime scene photos when he got a call from the morgue. They had finished the autopsy of the boy and the file was on the way.

"It's not on a disc, is it?" Ted said.

The doctor sounded confused as he said it was a standard file.

"All right, thanks. I'll call if I have any more questions."

As Ted hung up the phone, the doctor's assistant handed him the autopsy file.

The cause of death was a laceration to the throat. The killer drained blood from the body before dumping it into the river. No signs of abuse, trauma, or sexual activities. The autopsy of the boy from five years before stated the same cause of death. But police found that body in a lake on the other side of town.

"Viv, can you find out if there have been any cases like this in the last 25 years? I suspect it's the same killer from five years ago so I will follow a few leads from the old case. I also need to know how many rivers and lakes there are in the city."

Ted finally had a reason to get away from his desk for a while. He preferred field work to any other part of the job. Viviana was always better with the paperwork.

***

An old man and a little girl were walking along a dirty street. Usually called the bad side of town but with how hard it was raining no one wanted to be outside. The old man struggled to hold his umbrella while the little girl gripped his hand. They turned down an alley with nothing but trash and an overflowing dumpster.

"Where are we going?" the little girl said.

"You'll see soon enough. It's a place where I go to feel better."

"Will I feel better?"

"Oh, I think you will; I'll make sure of that. Now be quiet; no one can know we're here. It's a secret."

"Okay." The girl said.

The old man opened a door near the end of the alley to an abandoned building. The little girl was getting more frightened with each step. Down the end of the hall was a door with a dim light shining through the cracks. The old man opened the door to reveal a room with candles and pieces of cloth all over the floor. Mountains of stuffed animals filled the room. Each one was something different, but they all looked similar. An animal smiling, looking pleasant.

"Everyone looks so happy here, don't they?" The old man said.

She nodded.

"Well, let me show you something."

The old man picked up and took the outside of the animal off to reveal a white ghost version of the animal with a frown.

"They're sad. They pretend to be happy on the outside because they're scared to tell anyone how sad they are. Do you know what that's like?"

The little girl nodded again as she wiped the tears from her eyes.

"Would you like to help all the animals not be sad anymore?"

She nodded and got very excited.

"If you help my friends here than I can help you not be sad. Would you like that?"

The old man held the little girl's chin as she smiled in agreement.

"I don't want to be sad anymore." The little girl said.

"Well, to help our friends, we have to let their ghosts out. We have to set them free so they can't get hurt anymore. There is only one way to let the Ghost inside out; to kill it."

The old man took a knife and offered it to the little girl. She was reluctant.

"Isn't killing wrong?"

The old man thought for a moment and then smiled.

"Killing is terrible, but if we don't take their life then they'll go back home to their daddy. A daddy that hurts them and touches them when their mommy's not around."

The little girl cried again.

"They don't want to go back to their daddy."

She sat down on her knees and continued to weep.

The old man kneeled down next to her.

"Everything will be all right my child."

He picked her head up and cut her throat with one fast swipe.

"No one can hurt you anymore. I've saved you."

***

It was an unproductive day for Ted. Every lead he investigated was a dead end. There were no witnesses to his

50

current case. No one remembered anything about the murder from five years ago. He spent the entire rainy afternoon questioning people with no luck.

Viviana found no similar cases. Not even in the surrounding states.

"Maybe the cases don't have a connection." She said.

"There are too many similarities. The age and gender of the victim, the MO of the killer, it's no coincidence."

"How can you be sure? What if it's a copycat?"

"It's not a copycat."

"But how do you know?"

"I know!" Ted said.

"I don't understand why you can't consider the possibility."

"I'm not considering the possibility because I know it's the same killer."

"But how do you know?"

Ted felt too frustrated to answer the question. Many of their conversations were like this. Each of them getting annoyed and making no progress to a conclusion. Neither of them would admit that their prior relationship had leftover baggage.

The argument didn't stop either of them from doing their job. It helped push them harder to solve the case. Ted spent most of the evening driving up and down the river. He caught one man attempting to dispose of buckets filled with human feces.

Viviana was trying to identify the body. No missing children matched the description. Despite the argument, she knew Ted was usually right with his assumptions. The five-year-old murder never identified the body either. She thought Ted was right.

Ted spent the next day trying to identify the body with a photo from the morgue. Viviana had left a note on his desk; she rarely worked on Sundays. The note read no one had yet identified the bodies. Missing children usually get reported immediately. It was odd that the body matched none of the missing children. According to the autopsy report, the boy was dead for at least two days.

It was another long day with no progress. No one anywhere within 10 miles of the river had ever seen the boy. Ted believed the killer drove a great distance to dispose of the body. They couldn't do anything else until Monday morning. He left a note for Viviana to fax the photo to all the local schools hoping to identify the boy. He never went to work on time, and this was something that needed done first thing in the morning. Viviana never complained about when he worked. She wanted to avoid an unnecessary fight. And because he usually worked 12 hours a day and never took a day off. He was the most successful detective, so she gave him a little slack as long as he continued to show results.

Ted awoke to his phone ringing. It was an hour before his usual wake time.

"Why the hell is she calling me at 9:30 in the morning?"

He knew it was Viviana. She was the only one who ever called him.

"What!?"

"Hey Ted, sorry to wake you."

She sounded sincere.

"Did you get an ID on the boy?"

"No, nothing yet. I'm calling because there's another body in the river; a little girl this time."

"Where?"

"Off Third Street. McKenzie has the area secured. He's waiting on the ME, but you should be able to make it in time if you leave now."

"All right I'm on my way."

This was one of the few occasions that Ted didn't mind getting woken up early. Ted even found the taste of coffee to be more desirable when he was sleep deprived. It would only be a ten-minute drive. He took the time to make an extra pot of coffee to take with him. He felt this would be an even longer day than the others.

The man who found the girl's body was the same one who Ted had caught a couple days earlier. He was a thin older man with a long unkempt beard and was wearing a NASCAR t-shirt. This time he was out to catch crayfish and since he had no buckets of feces with him, the officers believed him. They were asking their final questions when Ted drove up.

"Why were you out fishing on a Monday morning?"

"Well, I sure as hell ain't gonna fish on a Sunday morning when I should be in church."

"I mean shouldn't you be at work?"

McKenzie was getting frustrated.

"I take Sundays and Mondays off and work the other days."

"Where do you work?"

"Triple A Fence down on Western Ave."

He was proud of this statement.

"That's all we have for now. We may need to ask you more questions later but you're free to go."

"Is it all right if I fish down the way?"

"As long as you're passed the caution tape you can fish all you want." Ted said.

The old man picked up his fishing pole and tackle-box and marched down the river for a good spot to sit. The ME had arrived and was already examining the body. McKenzie didn't wait for Ted to ask questions. He hadn't been with the police force long. His military training had taught him preparedness and to expect anything.

"The old man found her about an hour ago. He saw no one, but it looks like she's been here for at least a few hours."

Despite being a military man, McKenzie couldn't handle the sight of a corpse.

"More like a couple days. What's the time of death, Doc?"

"You always seem to ask me right as I find out myself. I'd say it was between 10 a.m. and 2 p.m. Saturday."

Ted felt uneasy. He didn't like having two unsolved murders in one week.

"So far it looks the same as the little boy, but we expect to get more details since the body hasn't been in the water as long."

The ME helped his assistant finish getting the stretcher ready for the body. They still had to wait for the officer to finish with the crime scene photos.

Ted overlooked the area. He looked at every piece of evidence. There was not much to see. He wandered around to see if he could find something someone might have missed. He saw something on the side of the river. He picked it up with the end of his pen he kept in his shirt pocket. It looked like the material found inside a stuffed animal. He called one officer over to photograph the material. He gave the crime scene one last look. The ME was putting the body in the ambulance. The animal stuffing was new, but it would be several hours before he would know any details about it. Sometimes he wished he could do the testing himself.

He still had a lot of paperwork but when he got back to the department, Viviana was looking for him.

"I got off the phone with McKenzie. He says it looks like the last murder. Are they related?"

"It looks that way, but we got something new on this one. There was what looks like material from a stuffed animal. I'm waiting to hear what the lab has to say about it."

"What are you thinking?"

"I'm thinking I need more information and won't have it for several hours. I need leads, Viv."

"Go home and rest. I'll call you when I have the autopsy report."

"You know I can't sleep when I'm in a dead spot on a case."

"I know, I'm asking you to try."

"In all the years we've worked together you still don't understand how I work."

"There are things you don't know about me either."

"Like how you want to control everyone instead of letting them do the work."

"Is it wrong that I try to help the officers working under me?"

"Is it if you never let them work? George used to say the same thing about his marriage with you."

Ted could see he hit a sore spot with her. He was only trying to make a point. He was not trying to upset her. As he was about to apologize; she spoke first.

"I'm not asking, I'm telling you, go home and rest. And never mention my ex-husband again."

Ted had never heard Viviana get so upset before. Something more than mentioning her ex was setting her off, but he did not know what. He decided not to argue and went home.

***

The old man walked for quite a while. He smiled at everyone he passed. He made small talk with comments like "Beautiful day!" or "Trying to stay active." No one knew his

55

true purpose. He walked past schools and parks, looking for the one child off away from the other children.

He saw one in a school playground. The other children were making fun of the little girl. She looked at the old man.

He smiled through the fence and told the little girl, "Don't listen to them. They're only jealous because you're so pretty."

The little girl gave him a dirty look and ran inside. A little disappointed, he returned to his walk.

His next stop, a few blocks later, was a small park. These children were much younger than children he usually spoke with; the ones too young to be in school. He saw a young boy poking at the ground with a stick. He was older than the other children. Remaining by the fence, the old man called to him.

"Young man? You there, young man?"

The little boy looked up at him confused. The old man continued.

"Hello. Shouldn't you be in school?"

The little boy shook his head still looking confused.

"Oh! Well you're almost a man; I thought you'd be in school."

"I was but my mommy didn't like me being in the special classes. She said I don't need special classes because I'm like all the other kids."

The child seemed unhappy with his mother's claim.

"Well, I agree you look special."

"Okay."

The old man thought this was a strange reply.

"Hey mister? Why do you walk funny?"

"Oh, that's from an old injury I had many years ago."

"Joey!"

The little boy's mother called him.

"There you are. Have you been behind this tree the whole time? I'm sorry; I hope he wasn't bothering you."

"Not at all, he was asking about why I limp."

The old man smiled.

"Come on sweetie, it's time to go home."

"Oh."

The little boy looked disinterested.

The old man walked slower watching the mom and the little boy. He saw them get into a dark green sedan and memorized the license plate number. He was curious about the boy. He differed from the other children.

***

Despite his many efforts, Ted could not calm his mind long enough to fall asleep. He could only lie in his bed staring at the ceiling. He forwent any further attempts and sat up. He rubbed his eyes wishing he had slept even a few minutes. He noticed a picture frame face down on his desk. He had laid it down over a year ago, but he still knew what photo it contained.

Something compelled him to look at it. He picked it up. He and Viviana embraced each other in the photo. He remembered the great time they had that night. He never was one for photos before or after this one. Ted felt he had not been happy since that photo. It was a short time later Viviana and her husband got divorced. She said nothing but Ted always felt it was his fault. He wondered if that was why she always seemed to push him harder than the other detectives. It was a few months after her divorce when she got promoted and moved to Ted's department.

He put the frame face down again and went to the kitchen, still rubbing his face. He noticed the coffee was black sludge in the pot and rinsed it out to make a fresh pot. He had to move several dirty dishes out of the way to complete his task. There were more dishes on his stove than in his sink. He was about to dry the cleaned pot when the phone rang.

"Yeah?"

"Hey Ted. Did I wake you?"

Viv was trying to sound warm and gentle.

"No, I was about to make coffee. Tell me you have some good news."

"I got the autopsy report. The girl had some of that stuffing in her hand. It matches what you found at the crime scene."

"That might only mean she had a stuffed animal or something when someone abducted her."

"There's more good news, someone identified her. The parents are coming in now to confirm the body."

"Awesome! I'll be there in about thirty minutes."

"Before you go, were you able to sleep?"

Ted thought about the photo on his desk.

"I got a couple hours. I'll see you soon."

He hung up before she could respond. Flusters of emotion were coming back to him and he wanted to get them under control. He still cared for her, but no one would have noticed with the way they had treated each other the last couple of months.

He was not sure exactly what he was feeling. The end of his relationship with Viv was abrupt. She gave no explanation and Ted never asked. They did not speak for months. He assumed it was a fling and moved on until Viv got promoted to Sergeant and made his supervisor.

He wondered if he had held some resentment towards her. He was a little nicer and tried not to argue with her as much. By the time he made it back to the precinct, he was in a good mood. The other officers gave him strange looks.

"Have the parents arrived yet?" Ted said.

"They're going down to the morgue now." Viv said.

58

"Outstanding! Let's go solve this case."

Ted clapped his hands and seemed to have a little pep in his step.

"You're in a good mood. I should send you home to nap more often."

Viv was expecting a sarcastic reply. Ted half smiled and continued walking to the elevator. She was not sure whether to feel happy or concerned about his sudden change in character.

When they arrived in the morgue, the parents had confirmed the child's body with the Medical Examiner. A young officer was escorting them out of the room. The mother was holding her mouth trying to suppress her loud sobbing. The father was a few steps behind her fighting with his emotions to stop the tears that were rolling down his face. Ted tried to be delicate so they would not be angry with him for asking questions.

"Mr. and Mrs. Stevens? I'm Detective Riggins, this is Sergeant Ledesma. If you're not feeling up to answering questions, I can give you my card and we can set up a time tomorrow?"

Mr. Stevens nodded but said nothing. He had an empty look in his eyes. Mrs. Stevens still sobbing, spoke up.

"We can talk now. I want the bastard that did this found!"

Ted spoke with his stern questioning voice that Viv admired.

"You reported your daughter, Emily, missing two days ago. The report states you hadn't seen or heard from her for three days. Why did you wait so long to file the report?"

"The last time we saw her, my husband, and I were drinking, and we got into an argument. We threw things, but no one got hurt. We thought she ran off to a friend's house down the street like before."

59

"This wasn't the first time she ran off?"

"It's happened two or three times, but she was with people we knew. She always called the next day and would come home after a couple days. I got concerned when I didn't hear from her, so I called everyone in the neighborhood. No one had seen her, and I filed the report."

"It's all my fault! I said horrible things I didn't mean. She'd still be here if I hadn't said those things." Mr. Stevens said.

"What did you say?" Viv said.

"I said my daughter was a burden. I made my baby girl run away and now she's dead."

Mr. Stevens walked away.

"I don't blame my husband or myself, but if we had reported her missing sooner, she'd still be alive."

"Did Emily have any stuffed animals she would take with her?"

Ted was writing on his notepad as he spoke.

"Um, no. We never bought her any. She never seemed to care for them."

"Thank you, Mrs. Stevens. We'll let you know if we have more questions."

"Detective? There was a little boy who disappeared from our neighborhood a few years ago. Do you think this happened to him?"

"I wouldn't know, ma'am."

Ted walked away. He stopped.

"How old was that little boy, Mrs. Stevens?"

"He was about six years old. Why?"

"I'll check missing persons about the boy."

Ted went back to the elevator, his mind racing.

"I'll bet that's the boy's body from five years ago." He said.

"Are you sure?"

"No. The body floated in the water for several weeks. Fish and other animals had eaten most of the identifiable parts. If we can get the missing boy's dental records, we can cross check it with the body."

"You still think it's the same killer."

"Yep! You always said I had a one-track mind."

Viv snorted at Ted's comment.

"It's funny." He said.

"What's that?"

"I forgot what it was like; not to argue with you all the time."

Viv looked at him a little puzzled. He raised his eyebrows returning the gaze. The elevator door opened. She found it difficult not to smile as she walked.

***

The old man was clever. With a description of the green sedan and the license plate number, all he needed to do was ask around. He developed the ruse that the little boy had left a stuffed animal at the park and wished to return it. With a reputation as a polite old man, everyone was happy to help him. It did not take long before he knew where the boy lived. He learned the boy's name and the mother's name. He even heard about the dispute the mother had with the local school.

He made his way to the boy's home to verify it was the correct place. As he passed, he heard raised voices. The boy seemed to shout, and the mother was trying to quiet him. The front door opened, and the boy shouted back inside.

"I'm playing outside; I'll stay in the front yard."

He slammed the door and sat on the porch, holding his head in his hands.

"How strange."

He watched the boy for a moment. He looked in the window and saw the mother standing with a blank expression. There was a phone ring, and the mother went to answer. The old man took his opportunity.

"Hello young man."

The boy looked up. The old man waved at him.

"Hi."

The boy looked confused.

"You forgot something at the park."

"What?"

The old man revealed a stuffed animal. It was a platypus.

"This is Paul." The old man said.

"Oh."

The boy looked disinterested.

"Well, you can have him. Do you want him?"

"My mommy won't let me keep him. She won't let me have things I want."

"You'll like him. Let me show you something."

The old man pulled material off the platypus. The inside was white, and the face was dark and sad. It was a ghostly-looking platypus.

"You see? Paul's sad too."

"Why is he sad?" The boy said.

"Paul's mother doesn't love him, and he has no friends. Would you like to be his friend?"

The boy looked at Paul for a moment. He glanced back at his house to see if his mother was watching.

"You don't have to tell your mom about him. Then you can keep him as long as you want, okay?"

"Okay."

The old man covered up the platypus and handed it to the boy.

"You take good care of him now and I'll come and see you tomorrow, okay?"

"Okay."

The boy hid the stuffed toy under his shirt and ran back inside. The mother was still on the phone as the old man made his way down the sidewalk whistling a cheerful tune.

***

Ted spent a little time talking to the cold case detectives. He needed to know what they had done to identify the body.

"I'll be honest, Ted, I pushed that one to the side and worked on cases I knew I could solve. The only option I saw for identifying the body was with dental records."

"Why didn't you try?"

"You could spend six months cross checking all the records in the city with that boy's and still never identify him."

"If I bring in a couple dental x-rays, could you see if there's a match?"

"Yeah, a couple would be easy."

"Okay, I got a hunch, we'll see if I'm right. Thanks Frank."

Ted only wanted one set of records checked but if his coworker agreed to a couple, then he'd have no complaints with one. This all depended on whether he could get any records. He got the address from the missing person's report and hoped he could get the records. It was still early in the evening so Ted thought he would not have trouble speaking to the family.

When he arrived at their home, he saw through the window they had finished dinner. He made a quick scan of the neighborhood. Other than a woman walking her dog, the street was quiet as the sun was setting. He rang the doorbell and waited. He heard a dog bark from inside and then turning of the deadbolt on the door.

"Can I help you?"

A man answered the door looking perplexed and worried.

"I'm Detective Riggins. Are you Mr. Lewis?"

Ted revealed his badge to verify his title.

"Yes, I am. Is something wrong?"

"Not in the way you're thinking. Do you have a moment to answer a few questions?"

"Yes. Please come in."

Ted followed Mr. Lewis into the living room. A woman, whom Ted assumed was Mrs. Lewis sat on the couch holding the collar of a Great Dane. She was petting the animal as a snarl grew on its face.

"Detective Riggins would like to ask us some questions. This is my wife."

"Mrs. Lewis."

"So, how can we help you, Detective?"

"A few years ago, we discovered the body of a young boy we could never identify. I don't want to get your hopes up, but it could be your son."

"Oh My God!"

Mrs. Lewis placed her hand on her chest and moved it to her mouth as she cried. Mr. Lewis was skeptical.

"But you're not sure? Why tell us? Why get us excited and emotional?"

"I came to ask if you had any of your son's dental records so we could verify if it is his body or not."

"I'll get them right now."

Mrs. Lewis ran to another room with the Great Dane following her.

"I'm sorry, Detective. How I acted was rude."

"It's all right Mr. Lewis."

"So, if this is our son, was he kidnapped? I always thought he ran away."

"Why is that?"

"We had recently moved here, and Billy had no friends. He missed his old friends and was furious with us. We called all his friend's parents, but they never saw him. We stopped searching about two years ago but hoped he would come back."

Mrs. Lewis returned with the dog at her feet.

"These are his entire medical records, Dental, everything."

"You understand I'm not making promises. This may not be your son."

"I understand."

Tears still fell from her face.

"I'll return these as soon as possible."

"Thank you, Detective. I'll show you out."

Mr. Lewis walked Ted to the door. The dog barked as the door shut and Ted returned to his car, thoughts running through his mind. He wondered why he never thought of this all those years ago when they first found the unidentified body. There were not any leads the last time. There were hundreds of missing children to cross reference. He hoped these records would match.

Ted dropped off the dental records with Frank and then got the missing person's report for the little boy. The last person to see him was an elderly man who lived down the street from the parents. If the dental records were a match, he would go talk to the old man.

Viviana approached his desk and threw a large stack of papers at him. The bags under her eyes displayed the exhaustion that Ted sometimes felt. She did not look angry but didn't look pleased either.

"Since you've been in a better mood lately, you think you can finish these reports? You're two weeks behind and the Lieutenant has been riding my ass."

"Yeah, I'll work on it right now."

"What? You're serious?"

"Yeah. I'm waiting to hear about the dental records on the boy we couldn't identify six years ago."

Viviana still looked surprised as the phone on Ted's desk rang.

"That might be Frank now. Riggins. Hey Frank, any luck? You're sure? Good, I've got a lead on something, can you notify the parents? Thanks, I owe you one. Come on. We gotta talk to an old man."

"Okay, what about?"

"I'll explain on the way."

Ted drove back to the neighborhood with Viv. He explained everything he knew. She listened. A long time passed since he spoke all his thoughts to her. Ted stopped in front of the address he got from the report for the old man. It was dark now, but the home sat illuminated with one front light by the door and a small light on the brick mail box.

Viviana spoke, stopping Ted from getting out of the car.

"So, what's with this change in you?"

"I don't know, I thought it was time for a change."

"At some point we should talk. About… about what happened between us."

"You mean… you mean now? I agree we should talk but some other time."

***

The old man was patient. He observed his prey from across the street, hiding in the bushes. He felt accustomed to this. Watching and waiting several days for the right opportunity. He did not expect the opportunity to come too soon.

He watched the boy go out into the yard. The boy sulked and dragged his feet. He was unhappy about something and the old man wondered what was bothering him. The mother walked out with her purse on her shoulder and keys in her hand. The old man listened.

"Make sure you pick up all your toys in the yard and wash up for dinner. I'll be back in about ten minutes; I need to pick up butter from the store."

"Yes, mommy."

The mother stroked the little boy's hair, but he pulled away. She held her hand in the air for a moment and took a deep breath. She turned towards the car.

"I'll be right back, sweetie."

"Okay, mommy."

The old man had moved out of the bushes by now, acting as if he were walking down the sidewalk. He knew no one would think it was unusual for him to be walking two streets down from his own. He waved to the mother as she waved back. He wondered if she remembered seeing him in the park. As the green sedan turned the corner, the old man crossed the street to the little boy.

"Would you like help with that, young man?"

The little boy continued his task and did not look up to answer.

"No, thank you."

"Well, you got a lot of toys to pick up. You and your friends must've had fun."

"I have no friends." The little boy said.

"Oh, I'm sorry to hear that. Well, you still have Paul, don't you? Isn't he your friend?"

"My mom took him away."

"Why'd she do that?"

"She was mad at me."

"Why was she mad?"

The boy shrugged his shoulders. He had stopped picking up toys.

"Would you like to go on a walk with me? I thought we could be friends."

"My mom would get mad again."

"I'll speak to your mom when she comes back. It'll be okay."

The boy stared for a moment.

"Okay."

***

Ted and Viv continued their conversation as they exited Ted's car.

"I didn't mean right now but we need to talk at some point." Viv said.

"We'll talk after this."

They passed the gate when a neighbor caught their attention.

"You folks looking for the old man that lives here?"

"Yes sir, I'm Detective Riggins and this is Sergeant Ledesma. We need to ask Mr. Noone a few questions."

"He usually walks around the neighborhood in the evenings. He should be back sometime soon."

"Thank you. Have you been his neighbor long?"

"Not long, a few months. I never knew his name until you told me."

"You don't know him that well?" Viv said.

"No. Is he in some kind of trouble?"

"We need to ask him a few questions."

Viv heard something on the police radio in Ted's car. Ted walked back towards the front door of the house.

"Ted, we got an Amber Alert two blocks from here. This is Sergeant Ledesma and Detective Riggins responding to Amber Alert. Over."

"What is your location, Sergeant? Over."

"Two blocks away, we're almost there. Over."

Ted got in the car as Viv finished speaking.

"Which way?"

"Turn left up here. Then turn right at the next street."

As they rounded the final corner, they saw a woman pacing the street. When she saw Ted and Viv, she waved her arms and jumping up and down. Ted stopped next to her.

"Did you call about the missing child?"

"Yes! My son is missing. I left for ten minutes and when I came home, I couldn't find him. A neighbor said they saw him walking with an elderly man, but he wouldn't walk off with anyone."

"Did they say which way the elderly man took your son?"

"I don't know."

She turned around to call for the neighbor.

"Steve? Steve! Which way did they go?"

A man sitting on his porch pointed in the direction Ted was driving.

"All right, ma'am, we'll have a patrol car come wait with you. We'll drive down and see if we can find your son."

"What's your son's name?" Viv said.

"His name is Joey. He's seven-years-old, short dark brown hair. He's wearing a striped polo shirt with jeans."

"Do you know anything about the elderly man?"

"They didn't see him, but Joey said an old man gave him some stuffed animal earlier today."

"We'll find him! That's our guy."

"The Richardson River is about a mile from here, isn't it?" Viv said.

"Yep."

"Where do you think he's taking the boy?"

"Not to his home. Isn't there an abandoned warehouse near hear?"

"Yeah."

"Send officers over to check it out. I gotta hunch."

"You sure about this one."

"No, but my hunches are usually right so let's try it."

They drove through several neighborhoods asking people if they had seen the boy and the old man. One woman said she saw them get on a bus heading towards the river. The warehouse was in the same direction. The dispatcher confirmed that units were already at the warehouse. Ted passed one bus on the way but couldn't see the boy on it. They got to the warehouse and waited. Officers found a vehicle registered to the old man. This gave them probable cause to enter the warehouse.

"You think this is a good time to talk? About us?" Ted said.

"No. We can talk when this case is over."

Viv wanted to talk uninterrupted. It was important, but the child had priority.

They could see the first bus in the distance. They waited.

***

The old man considered reaching to hold the boy's hand but thought it best not to. The boy walked alongside him with his hands in his pockets. He watched his feet as they trampled over the discolored wet leaves on the sidewalk.

"What's your name, young man?"

The old man tried to remain causal and friendly. It was too soon to enact his true desires.

"Joey. What's your name?"

"You can call me Mr. Noone. Joey's a good name. I had a nephew named Joey."

"Had? You mean he died."

"Yes, a long time ago. He drowned in his family's swimming pool. It was a tough time for everyone. He was about your age. And like you, he didn't get along with his

70

parents. I gave him a stuffed bear the day before he died. I'm sorry; I'd rather not talk about this."

"What do you want to talk about?"

"Well, what sort of things do you like to talk about?"

"I don't know. I don't talk much." Joey said.

"It seems like you have lots of things to say."

"Yeah but many people don't listen because I'm only a kid."

"Nonsense. I'm listening right now."

"Okay."

Joey's response confused Mr. Noone. He saw a bus rattling down the street. This was the right time.

"Would you like to go to my shop and pick out another toy? I have too many. You can have as many as you want. You can even get one for your mom."

The old man was anxious. He did not want to miss the bus.

"Okay."

Joey's response sounded melancholy, but he did not hesitate to get on the bus with Mr. Noone.

"If we leave now, we can go where we want and get you back home in time for supper."

"What's supper?" Joey said.

"I suppose you call it dinner."

"Oh."

The bus ride seemed longer than it was. After only fifteen minutes, they had arrived where Mr. Noone looked out the window and sat back down. He didn't want to get off the bus.

"Shouldn't be much longer now." Mr. Noone said.

One person paid the fair and found a seat close to the front of the bus. Another person stepped up and spoke to the bus driver. Everyone looked forward to see what was happening. The man who spoke to the bus driver turned towards the passengers.

"My name is Detective Ted Riggins. I'm looking for a young boy named Joey."

"My name is Joey."

The little boy stood up next to Mr. Noone.

"What's your mother's name, Joey?" Detective Riggins said.

"Lily."

"Your mother is outside Joey. She'd like to see you."

"Okay."

"Is that the man you got on the bus with?" Detective Riggins said.

"Yes."

Detective Riggins looked at Mr. Noone.

"Could you come with me, Sir?"

"I hope there's no trouble. I was on my way to an old friend's for the evening."

"We'll talk about it outside. Watch your step, Sir."

Mr. Noone saw Joey get in to the back of a police car. The boy did not understand what was happening. Mr. Noone did not know what was happening. How did the police get here so fast?

"What were you doing with the young boy, Sir?" Detective Riggins said.

"I met him at the bus stop. He wouldn't tell me where his parents were, so I thought I would look after him on the bus."

Despite his lie, Mr. Noone seemed calm and relaxed.

"May I see your identification please?"

"Oh, yes, Detective."

Mr. Noone noticed Joey speaking to a woman. He thought she might be another detective.

"Is this your current address, Mr. Noone?"

"Yes, Sir."

"You met the boy at the bus stop. Have you ever seen him before?"

"Not that I can recall, no."

"One last question, Mr. Noone, have you ever seen this girl before?"

Detective Riggins showed a photo of a young brunette girl. The same girl Mr. Noone had spent an evening with in the same warehouse he was planning to take Joey.

"Well, I don't see how that is relevant, but no I've never seen her."

"Someone murdered this girl last week. Witnesses say she was last seen with an elderly man matching your description. This girl lived down the street from you; two blocks south of where Joey Devereux lives. Are you sure you've never seen her before?"

Mr. Noone's right hand shook. He moved it behind his back hoping the Detective would not notice.

"Yes–yes I'm sure. How could I n-n-know everyone who lives on my street?"

The perspiration on his face was showing. He wiped it off with his shaking hand.

"I-I-I-I don't feel well. I would like to have a little water."

Mr. Noone walked off muttering to himself.

"Wait a minute, Mr. Noone. Mr. Noone!"

Detective Riggins had little time to blink before the old man struck him in the face. The Detective did not flinch and continued his struggle with the old man. He broke free before other officers could aid the Detective.

"Freeze!"

The old man didn't listen.

"FREEZE!"

The old man continued charging towards Joey. He was a few feet away when the female detective stepped between them with her pistol directed at Mr. Noone.

"One more step and there'll be a hole in your brain."

Mr. Noone dropped to his knees and sobbed.

"I wanted to save him. He is unhappy. He needs me to release him. Like the others."

"Does that sound like a confession to you Sergeant Ledesma?" Detective Riggins said.

"Yes Detective, it does."

She looked at Joey.

"Are you ready to go home?"

"Yes, ma'am."

Joey thought for a moment.

"Is he a bad man?"

Sergeant Ledesma smiled.

"I think he believed he was a good man."

"Oh."

"Joey!"

Joey's mother picked him up, hugging him as tight as she could.

"My baby. Are you hurt?"

"You're squeezing me too hard."

Detective Riggins fought back a laugh. Sergeant Ledesma backhanded him in the chest.

"The boy's Autistic."

"That doesn't make what he said less funny."

She slapped him again.

"Owe! Stop it."

"What if you had an autistic child?"

Detective Riggins thought for a moment.

"I'd still think the boy's comment was funny. Besides, it's not like I'll be having children in the foreseeable future."

Sergeant Ledesma scoffed and walked away.

"You almost did."

Detective Riggins smiled. A realization of horror creeped upon his face.

"What? You mean when you and I… well what happened? Viv?"

"It doesn't matter. It was before my divorce."

"Is that why you've been so hard on me since you made Sergeant?"

She smiled.

"A little."

Mr. Noone heard nothing after they put him in the police car. He sat, hands cuffed behind his back, trying to think of where he made his mistake. The driver of the police car turned the flashing lights off. They turned the street corner and faded into the darkness of the city.

Creatures Exhibit

Creatures has a broad definition. For the sake of our exhibit and this museum, creature refers to anything that is not human. There are some which were born as creatures and create death wherever they go. Others have a sort of death and are born again as creatures. With humans and creatures, many situations cause them to be reborn. Where there is birth there is death. Death is always around us and is not always something bad, dark, or scary.

Many stories are well suited for this exhibit, but rest elsewhere. When origins are unknown. When they have a natural occurrence. When their reality comes into question, we place them in this exhibit. You may see creatures in many of our other exhibits. The creatures may not be the focal point of the collection or piece. As the curator, I choose the pieces for each exhibit. I've often received feedback on my choices. Sometimes I discuss changes. Sometimes I do not. A year from now I may alter the exhibits, or I'll leave them as they are.

The museum is a living, growing thing. In a way, it's a kind of creature. Nothing is permanent. The museum has experienced many changes. It's had many deaths and rebirths. It's as much a story as all those within its walls. Come see the creatures within the creature. You've paid your admission. Now wander the halls, study and learn of creatures and death. You may see a glimpse of yourselves, but don't let it frighten you. Learn from it and grow. Become something better inside the Creatures Exhibit.

The Harpy of Miller Road

The following are transcriptions of recordings from the Kay County Sheriff's Department. The Kay County Administration Building holds archived copies of the original recordings. The archives are in the records department on the second floor.

***

911 Call placed on 11 June 2016, 00:14

Dispatch – 911 What is your emergency?

Caller – I'm on Miller Road south of Ponca City and there is a naked woman walking down the road.

Dispatch – Stay on the line for the Kay County Sheriff's Department.

Caller – Thank you.

(thud thud)

Unknown – (muffled) Help Me!

Dispatch – Sheriff's Department, Hammond.

(thud thud)

Caller – I'm on Miller Road south of Ponca City and…

Unknown – Help Me!

Caller – …and there is a naked woman walking down the road.

Dispatch – Is she injured?

Caller – I don't think so. She's hitting my car window yelling 'help me.'

(thud thud)

Dispatch – We have a deputy on the way. Is she white, black, or Hispanic?

Caller – She's white. She's an elderly woman with long white hair.

Unknown – Help Me!

Caller – She's trying to get in the car, but I have the doors locked.

Dispatch – Remain in your car until the deputy arrives.

(door opens)

Caller – Oh my God!

Dispatch – Sir?

Unknown – Help Me!!

Caller – Let go of me!

Dispatch – Sir!?

(growling)

Caller – Oh God!

Dispatch – Sir? Are you okay? Sir?

(yelling and growling in distance, line disconnects)

***

"Case #1606110049 Date: 14 June 2016. Detective Nathan Gold Interviewing Deputy Donavan Mackey. Age 24. Kay County Sheriff's Department. Deputy Mackey, please start at the beginning. What happened?"

"I responded to a call on 11 June at approximately 00:45. A man had called about a nude elderly woman wandering around Miller Road asking for help. Dispatch said he waited in his car on the side of the road. The woman pounded on his window yelling 'help me.' It took a half hour to drive out there. When I arrived, I saw a vehicle with its hazard lights flashing but I saw no one in or around the vehicle. The passenger's side door sat open with the engine still running. I found a cell phone about ten feet from the car near the trees. I attempted to turn it on, but the battery was low. I notified dispatch of the situation and they sent out Deputy Jones and Deputy Swanson. They arrived about twenty minutes later. We searched through the tree line together but found nothing. I had the cell phone charging in my vehicle, and I determined that it was the phone that made the 911 call. The owner of the cell phone and the registered owner of the vehicle is Peter Tucci. He is a schoolteacher, and we later learned he was on his way to visit family for the weekend. His whereabouts are still unknown."

"Have there been any other calls or reports about this area?"

"Not since I joined the Sheriff's Department. There have been rumors and urban legends. Drivers claiming to have seen a nude elderly woman walking down that part of Miller Road. This is the first instance that I'm aware of someone making a call."

"Does anyone live near the area?"

"The closest house is about twenty minutes away; a family of four. They were all asleep at the time of the incident and claim they never heard or saw anything out of the ordinary."

"Did Mr. Tucci make any other calls that night?"

"The last call was to 911. Dispatch said the call disconnected."

***

"Case #1606110049 Date: 14 June 2016. Detective Nathan Gold Interviewing Dr. Arthur Hobbs. Age 54. Kay County History Museum. Dr. Hobbs what can you tell me about any folklore in Kay County about a nude elderly woman?"

"There have been several accounts in diaries, journals, and personal letters. There's one news article from the early Twentieth Century about this elderly woman. She only appears on Miller Road and only late at night. Most of the accounts are from passersby claiming to have seen this woman. She's always described in the same way. No one mentions an exact age or nationality. The description is always of a nude elderly woman. There have been three documented disappearances in Kay County in sixty years. Each person allegedly traveled down Miller Road. There is no evidence to support where they were traveling. Many have suggested it's a scam set up to rob the naïve but there are no accounts in surrounding counties. Others have suggested this elderly woman is an evil spirit collecting souls. My theory is this woman practices some ancient rituals and needs sacrifices for these rituals. There have been accounts of Occultists making human sacrifices to appease their Gods. But there's no evidence to support this."

"Is there a pattern in which these sightings of the woman occur?"

"I have seen no patterns. The recorded dates of these accounts seem at random over the years. There's no way to predict the next sighting."

***

"Case #1606110049 Date: 20 June 2016. Detective Nathan Gold reporting. There has been another sighting of the nude elderly woman on Miller Road. It is 22:33 and I am pulling up to the location of the sighting. The individual who reported the sighting continued driving. There is nothing in the area I can see from the road. I will wait to see if the woman reappears. There is still no pattern to any of the sightings."

***

"Case #1606202349 Date: 24 June 2016. Detective Sharon Stinson reporting. Police found Detective Nathan Gold's body on 20 June 2016 at approximately 23:49 on Miller Road. Cause of death was from loss of blood from many lacerations all over the body. There is no trace of blood around the crime scene. There were no signs of a struggle around the body suggesting someone moved it post mortem. The county closed off Miller Road pending the results of the investigation."

Disengagement

The room was a sullen gray with brutal fluorescent light raging down from the high ceiling. Nothing was on the walls except a long mirror on one side of the room. A long black table sat positioned in the room's center with only two chairs; one on either end. Peter Dominic sat alone, handcuffed with his head in his hands sobbing. As he sulked, trying to remember how the last few hours must have unfolded, a man and a woman entered the room. The woman carried a manila folder. Peter believed this folder contained everything that happened and personal information about him.

"Good evening, Mr. Dominic." The woman said.

The man who entered the room with her stood behind by the door.

The woman continued.

"My name is Detective Hartley. You know why you're here so why don't you tell me what happened."

"What was her name?" Peter said.

"I'm sorry?"

"The woman I… I killed. What was her name?"

Detective Hartley looked surprised. She looked through the file.

"Her name was Sarah Nicole Morris."

Peter wiped his eyes.

"Sarah Nicole Morris. Could you tell me about her? What did she do for a living? Did she have a family; children?"

Peter still felt upset about the incident. He was not a killer.

"She was studying at the community college to be a radiologist. She lived in an apartment with her boyfriend, they didn't have children."

Peter closed his eyes.

"Please tell the boyfriend I'm sorry."

Detective Hartley grew impatient.

"If you're sorry, why did you kill her?"

"I wasn't trying to kill her. I thought she was someone else; something else."

"What do you mean something else?"

"I don't know if what I saw was real or not. I'm not sure if I was being brainwashed or if I was hallucinating but I never wanted to hurt anyone. I never wanted to kill Sarah."

Peter sobbed and dropped his head back into his hands.

"Mr. Dominic?"

He didn't respond.

"Mr. Dominic?"

Detective Hartley felt Peter was playing her for a fool. She smacked the table causing Peter to jump.

"Tell me what happened. Why did you kill Sarah Morris?"

Peter wiped the tears off his face and cleared his throat.

"It was an accident. This all started in the morning on my way to work. I had finished eating breakfast and was about to leave."

***

"Thank you, sweetheart. I need to go now before I'm late."

Peter kissed his wife as he finished chewing the toast she made for him. He was double-checking his briefcase when the phone rang.

His wife answered.

"This is the Dominic's. Oh! Hello Jason. Peter was about to… I suppose he… all right hold on."

She covered the receiver with her hand.

"He needs to talk to you."

"Can't it wait until I get to the lab?"

Jason had never called him this early.

"He sounds upset. Something could be wrong."

Peter took the phone from her.

"Yes Jason? What!? No, nothing was unusual last night. Around four in the morning? You're sure? And it's already hit? Yes, I'll meet you at the sight. Okay. See you in about… twenty minutes."

Peter giggled as he closed his briefcase.

"What is it dear?"

"A meteorite landed last night outside of town. Jason got a call from the lab's security about all the instruments making loud noises. He's on his way out to the site now."

Peter couldn't contain his enthusiasm.

"That's wonderful Peter. Take lots of pictures for me."

She was always supportive of Peter's interests.

***

"I rushed out the door and drove ten miles over the speed limit all the way to the meteorite. This was something that excited and thrilled me and I was proud to be a part of it all."

Peter was silent for a long period.

"What kind of music do you think she listened too? What might her hobbies have been?"

Detective Hartley thought the only way to keep Peter talking was to tell him about who Sarah Morris was. She had information in the file but not a lot. She gestured to her partner to come closer and whispered in his ear. He left the room. The detective continued her questioning with a different approach.

"I will tell you what I can about Ms. Morris, but I need you to continue with your explanation Mr. Dominic."

"Have you ever killed anyone, Detective?"

"No."

"Then you don't understand how it feels to take someone else's life. It's sickening, like I may vomit. Please tell me something and I'll continue."

Peter said with hopeful eyes. Remorse was the only emotion he could display.

Detective Hartley sighed.

"She was five-nine and brunette with green eyes. She was very healthy and was a life guard volunteer with the YWCA."

"She sounds like my wife. Tell me more, please?"

"The more information you give me the more I give you."

Peter took a deep breath.

"When… when I arrived, Jason was taking samples. He was running tests to check for any radiation and magnetism. I couldn't believe how large the meteorite was…"

***

Jason had finished taping off the meteorite area. He tested radiation levels with his Geiger counter.

"Have you measured the impact area yet?" Peter asked as he walked down to the steaming rock.

"The impact area is about 30 meters in diameter. I haven't been able to measure the meteorite yet. It's still too hot."

Jason walked around the giant rock while observing the radiation readings.

"It's emitting radiation but not enough to be harmful. Can you get the magnet from my truck?"

Peter ran back up the hill for the magnet. He was about five feet away when the magnet jerked out of his hand and slammed against the meteorite. Peter and Jason were speechless and could only stare at the massive chunk of iron that stood as tall as they did.

Peter chipped off part of the rock. With very long gloves and a rock pick hammer, he gained a piece small enough to examine under a microscope. Jason remained with the meteorite to continue documenting data.

"This meteorite is unlike any I've encountered. We need as much data as possible."

"We should examine what we have collected for now and return tomorrow."

The extreme magnetism of the extra-terrestrial mass intrigued Peter.

"You go ahead; I'll keep working here. I want no one else taking credit for the find."

Jason seemed unaware of anything else that was going on. He always focused on his work, but his attitude became more obsessive within recent weeks. Peter knew he was going through a divorce. Ever since his wife caught Jason cheating on her, he only focused on work and didn't speak much. Peter went back to the lab to examine the samples from the meteorite.

***

"I felt uncomfortable leaving Jason by himself but paid no attention to my thoughts. I wanted to research the meteorite."

"I hope this is going somewhere Mr. Dominic, my patience is dwindling."

The detective was trying to push him to the important aspects of the day's events. Peter would tell the story his way. To him, all the facts were important.

"I promise this is all relevant. I had noticed the texture of the rock was unusual compared to other meteorites. This was smoother. It wasn't as dark as it should have been after hitting the atmosphere even though the sample was still warm. I was checking its magnetism strength when Jason called…"

***

Peter! We have to run! Get out of the lab now!
"Slow down. What are you talking about?"
No time! There's blood everywhere! They're coming for me!
"Jason? Who's coming for you? Jason!?"

Peter only heard a dial tone. He wondered what Jason could have been talking about. Could this have been a prank at his expense? Peter headed back to the meteorite site. Half way there, he noticed Jason's truck on the side of the road with the driver's side door left open.

"JASON!?"

There was no response. Peter looked around for footprints or tire tracks. There was nothing, not even tracks from Jason's truck. It looked like something picked up the truck and put in the dirt.

Peter jumped back into his car and continued on to the meteorite. He was not sure what to do. Should he call the police or find out if this was an elaborate prank?

***

Detective Hartley's partner returned with another file. He handed it to her and then resumed his position glaring at Peter with his stone-cold face.

"Would you like to know more about Ms. Morris?" She asked.

"Yes, please!"

Peter sounded sincere in his desire to learn about the woman he murdered.

"She volunteered with many children's organizations. She helped them overcome personal issues. She worked with overweight teenage girls. She enjoyed skiing and hiking. You

91

discovered your coworker Jason's truck, then what happened?"

"I headed back to the meteorite to find out what was going on…"

***

Peter found the site deserted. It looked as if Jason had left in a hurry. There were footprints that seemed to run in circles. Equipment looked as if someone dropped it and left it behind. It was unlike Jason to leave anything. This made Peter skeptical. Broken tape was lying around the meteorite, and it was no longer steaming. Peter placed his hand on it and noticed how cold it was.

Something ran through the trees as Peter walked past the crater. He didn't believe what his eyes saw at first. His mind must have been playing tricks on him; scaly skin with a dark complexion, thin and tall. He had to prove to himself that he didn't see this. He had to prove his mind was exaggerating his perception. He searched for the elusive figure. He wondered in circles around the forest for half an hour. He found nothing, and it was becoming difficult to see as the sun set into twilight. If there was something in the forest, Peter did not want to be alone in the forest at night.

He went back and looked for Jason by his truck. He made his way back to the truck, but the truck had gone. It looked as if the truck had come to a screeching stop but there was no sign of its departure. Peter was getting frightened, and he did not think this was a prank anymore. How did he not see the tire tracks before?

He drove to Jason's apartment, but no one was home. He checked the lab and found everything smashed. The meteorite samples were missing. With the phones broken, he went home and to call the police hoping Jason was waiting for him.

As he pulled into the driveway, Peter noticed another vehicle he had never seen before. It was a black, four-door sedan with plates from another state. Fear had created a lump in Peter's throat. He was not sure if his wife was home. He noticed the front door sat open and all the lights were off. It was dark now and usually his wife was watching television in the living room by this time. His heart beat faster. He called to see if anyone was home.

"Hello? Nikki, are you home?"

Nothing but silence filled the home. He searched the house. The kitchen, the bathroom and the backyard were all empty, so he went upstairs. As he neared the bedroom, he could hear what sounded like people fighting. Fearing his wife's life might be in danger, Peter ran to his study to get his pistol.

When he got back to the room, there was silence. He waited by the door. Nothing happened for a short time. His fear grew into courage and he opened the door. No one was there. He looked out the window but saw nothing. Thinking whoever it was may have jumped out the window he ran downstairs. He saw them in his backyard. With his heart still pounding, he believed what his eyes told him this time. Two dark figures with green slimy skin were running towards the garage. He aimed his pistol and fired two shots. One creature fell to the ground as the other continued running, cradling its arm. Peter chased after it.

The monster was in the black sedan before Peter could catch it. As it drove off, Peter got a good look at the scaly face. It had large black oval eyes, two small slits in place of the nose and a tiny thin mouth. Peter believed he had experienced a close encounter. This was the same creature he saw at the meteorite crater but refused to allow himself to believe it. His mind was reeling. What had happened to Jason? What had happened to his wife? Peter made his way back to the house to examine the other creature he had shot and killed.

He approached the body with the confidence of someone who had hunted a deer in the forest. He had conquered his prey and could rejoice in victory. He stopped. The body no longer looked like the creature he believed he had killed. Peter didn't understand. He was certain of what he had seen. Lying on the ground was a young woman, a brunette, with her face in the ground. She was dead with one shot to the torso. He had killed this young woman but did not know why she was in his home. He doubted what he had seen driving the black sedan. All he could do was drop to his knees and sob. He had taken a person's life and could not live with the guilt. He could hear the sirens echoing through the air. He was about to put the pistol in his mouth when someone shouted at him to drop the weapon.

***

"… and that's when the police arrived and brought me here."

Peter lowered his head again in shame and was silent. As he told the story, Detective Hartley was going through the file her partner had brought. With it open in front of her, she glared at Peter.

"Mr. Dominic, do you think I'm that naïve?"

"What?"

"Officers found you at the home of Jason Thomas. You told me it was your home."

Peter looked confused.

"No… no that is the house I bought with my wife."

"You're not married, Mr. Dominic. Try telling me the truth."

She was standing now.

"I have told you the truth. Every word was true to the best of my knowledge."

"Where is your coworker Jason Thomas?"

"I don't know."

"His reported his vehicle stolen this afternoon. Officers found it on the side of the highway as you said."

"Is he all right? Where is he?"

Peter was concerned. This was all confusing.

"The last place anyone saw him was at his home. The one you have claimed as your own."

Peter was getting angry.

"It is my home! I bought it with my wife!"

"You don't have a wife! Sarah Morris was your fiancée!"

"What!? I've never seen her before tonight!"

The confusion on Peter's face was genuine. He did not understand why Detective Hartley would make up facts.

"Let's see if we can jog your memory."

The detective slid a photo across the table. It was a photo of Peter with Jason on one side clapping and a girl who looked like Sarah Morris on his other side. Peter and Sarah were sitting close, half looking at each other. There was a banner in the background that read Happy Engagement.

"You two knew each other, Mr. Dominic. Jason Thomas was getting a divorce because he was having an affair with Sarah Morris. When you found out, you rushed over and killed her, but Jason got away, didn't he?"

Tears were rolling down Peter's face. He couldn't believe any of this.

"This is wrong! I don't remember her!"

"Officers found your fingerprints in Jason Thomas's vehicle. Can you tell me why your fingerprints were in his truck?"

"I've ridden in his truck before. Why wouldn't my finger prints be there?"

"Your prints were on the steering wheel."

95

"That's impossible!"

Peter was getting angry. He still didn't believe the photo was real.

"I've spoken to Jason Thomas. He said you're a manager at a video rental store. You've never worked in a lab."

"He's lying!"

"There have been no reports of any meteorites."

"SHUT UP! Why are you making this up? It all happened the way I said."

"See for yourself."

Detective Hartley flipped a switch on the wall beside the door. A light came on to reveal a room on the other side of the mirror. Jason Thomas sat alone, a sling around his left arm, despair written over his face.

As Peter looked at Jason's face, he remembered the events from that day. He had an argument with Sarah before going to work. She wanted him to find a better job. She said his life was not going anywhere. Living together had strained their relationship over the last few months. He received a phone call from Jason's ex-wife explaining the affair. In a bitter rage he stole Jason's truck and left it on the highway.

When he returned home in the evening, Sarah was not home. He assumed she was with Jason and hurried over to his home. He heard them both in Jason's bedroom. He kicked the door open screaming at them. They tried to reason with Peter and explain but he would not listen. In his blind anger, he grabbed Jason's pistol shouting threats. They ran and Peter fired the pistol only to frighten them. He never meant to kill anyone.

"Oh, God! What have I done?"

Peter cried trying to make sense of it all. Everything he thought had happened seemed so real.

Detective Hartley walked to the door and sighed. She looked at her partner.

"Get the doctor to look at him."

After the two detectives left, Peter looked up at Jason through the mirrored glass. Jason turned and looked at Peter. His face morphed into the creature Peter saw earlier that night. Peter screamed. He stumbled back into the corner of the room, stricken with fear and confusion. The light on Jason's side of the mirror shut off.

Clyde

As if he shifted places in a dream, Clyde found himself in a dark, small room. His surroundings looked unfamiliar. He gazed up and saw strange markings in the sky.

1 leveL

What is that? He thought.

He surveyed the room, which had only one small door. Others stood with him. Their complexions appeared different from his orange tone; one blue and one pink. They looked as confused as Clyde. The pink one nearest him spoke first.

"You must be new. Hi, I'm Pinky. What's your name?"

Clyde hesitated to answer at first. Something about the strange place made him feel uncomfortable.

"I'm...I'm Clyde. Do you know where we are?"

"We're about to start the mission. Special Ops stuff. You'll get the hang of it. Stick with Inky over here. He'll show you the ropes."

Pinky gestured to the blue fellow behind him. Inky seemed too nervous to speak and averted his eyes when Clyde looked at him.

The main door opened and another person, this one colored red, entered the small room. He looked angry and hardened from something that Clyde did not know. He had never seen anyone look so mean.

"I see you've all met the new recruit, Clyde. Welcome Private! I'm Blinky your Commanding Officer. You've met Pinky, my Lieutenant, and Inky, my Sergeant and your trainer for today. We're starting light for this exercise for the new guy's sake. Remember one thing Clyde. KILL THE YELLOW BASTARD!"

98

Blinky opened the door and ran off. The others followed and Clyde waited a moment.

Who or what is the Yellow Bastard?

He walked out with caution. He did not see anyone, but he could hear Blinky shouting.

"THERE HE IS! CHARGE!"

Clyde could only see a corridor. He turned to the right. There were several yellow pellets floating in the air at Clyde's eye level.

What are these puck things?

Every turn Clyde made only brought him more questions than answers. He saw a large cherry float by and decided to go back to the room he came from.

I don't want to know what's going on, this shit is too weird for me.

At that moment, he turned blue and started racing back towards the room. He could not understand why he changed or why he moved so fast. He began to enter the room when he saw a pair of eyes coming around the corner. They blinked and darted into the room. Clyde followed. Once in the room, the eyes grew a body around them. Inky, breathing fast and heavy. Clyde's body flashed white and blue than went back to his orange color.

"What the hell is going on?" Clyde said.

"There's a giant yellow creature that eats the yellow pellets. If he eats the big ones than he can eat us too but only for a short time. We have to kill him before he can eat us." Inky said.

"How are we supposed to do that?"

"Follow me."

Inky led Clyde out into the corridor again. There were heading to the left when Clyde saw the Yellow Bastard running down the other corridor. A giant ball with a huge mouth. It had sharp teeth protruding with slime and spit

99

dripping off them with tiny, beady black eyes. Blinky was right behind the monster shouting.

"PINKY!? FLANK HIM AT THE RIGHT!"

Clyde rounded the corner and saw where Pinky had hit the monster. It looked like the Yellow Bastard imploded.

I'm glad that's over.

"Get ready for the next one kid." Blinky said.

They all moved back to the room with one door.

"What next one?"

He looked up in the sky and saw the strange marking again. They looked a little different this time.

2 leveL

"LET'S GO!"

They all hurried out of the room again. Again, Clyde hesitated. He heard everyone shouting again. He rounded the corner at the end of the corridor. The Yellow Bastard charged towards him. He froze.

Shit!

The Hearing

The two security guards escorting him were more nervous than usual. They maintained their composure, but they walked faster down the white hallway. They passed numbered doors on either side. He was intimidating, this monster the security guards were escorting. They took him to a hearing which would determine if he could reintegrate back into society. He had committed no crimes, but his appearance made people uncomfortable. His tail wiggled up and down as they stopped by the door at the end of the hall: number 327.

The first guard knocked on the door while the second rested his hand on his weapon. The second guard kept his eyes on him while he tapped the claws on his left hand against his leg. A bead of sweat rolled down the second guard's face as he observed the monster's movements. A buzzer sounded signaling the door could open. The door revealed a large room with white walls and a grey floor. Frosted windows surrounded the room. They allowed light to enter but nothing was visible through the glass.

Three men sat behind a long table with a single chair placed in the room's center. The two security guards remained by the door as he walked to the solitary chair and sat down. The first man behind the table, the farthest to the left, was an old man. The old man resembled the grumpy dwarf from Snow White with his large nose and short stature. The gentleman in the middle was younger than the Grumpy Dwarf and more attractive. The last man on the far right, bearded and balding, was lying back in his chair with his arms crossed.

The attractive man cleared his throat as he spoke.

"Mmhm. Thank you, um, thank you for agreeing to meet with us today. We are here to discuss whether we should allow you to live amongst the public or remain segregated in your room. Away from other patients as you requested when you first arrived."

He was nervous as he spoke.

The grumpy dwarf jumped in.

"Does the monster have anything to say?"

The monster, he hated the term, glared at the grumpy man and halted swaying his tail. His voice was deeper than an average man's.

"My name is David Jones. I would appreciate it if you did not call me a monster."

He held his gaze on the grumpy man.

The attractive man continued, "I'm sorry Mr. Jones. Your doctors made us aware of how you feel about the term 'monster' and my colleagues and I will refrain from using it."

The attractive man made a quick glance to his right waiting for his neighbor's agreement.

"My name is Dr. Swanson. You've met Dr. Horowitz and to my left is Dr. Quaid. We have a few questions for you and please answer as honest as you can. First, could you tell us a little about your life before the incident?"

"My life before the incident is irrelevant, Dr. Swanson."

David seemed irritated by the doctor's question. The suit he was wearing was too small, but it was the only one David could find that almost fit. The pants tore a small amount at the seams as he sat down. He could never find clothes and shoes were not even an option. He could not contain the claws on his feet. He continued speaking to Dr. Swanson trying hard not to look at the grumpy dwarf.

"The last clear memories I have from my past were around the time of the incident that altered my appearance. This is where I'll begin."

"Go ahead Mr. Jones."

102

Dr. Swanson got his pen and pad ready. David was still avoiding Dr. Horowitz's gaze and Dr. Quaid still had not moved.

"The last moment I recall before the change was waking up inside a large cage at the back of a tiny warehouse. A great deal of chemical equipment and laboratory machinery filled the room. The dusty wooden floor and many large wooden beams overhead gave me an uneasy feeling. This was more disconcerting than the cage containing me. I was alone for a long duration. I surveyed my surrounding; seeking a possible escape route. Unfortunately, I could not find one in enough time before my captors returned.

"As they entered, they seemed to argue about something, but I couldn't decipher their words. They noticed that I was awake, and this seemed to upset them. I tried to speak, but I could not. I still could not understand what they were saying as they approached me. I may have still been under the influence of whatever drug or tranquilizer they gave me when they took me. The younger of the two men grabbed my arm and inserted a needle, injecting me with some kind of green liquid. A moment later everything was black.

"The next time I awoke, my body was in severe pain. The pain was blinding. When the transformation was complete, the pain had subsided, and I could only lie on the cage floor. Dizziness came over me and I grew furious. Rage took control of me and I bent the cage bars with ease. I was throwing desks and tables all over trying to locate a way out of my prison. I finally saw a window twenty feet above me and climbed the wall to escape. In my rage, I did not notice if the two men were around to see my primitive tantrum. I ran off into the darkness of the city taking cover within the

103

sewers. I hadn't noticed my change of appearance until several hours later."

Dr. Swanson and Dr. Horowitz were taking many notes as David spoke. The bald man continued his gaze on David never moving or flinching. David wondered if he was in fact alive. David could hear the two security guards fidgeting as they stood near the door. They were still nervous around David.

"How long did you live down in the sewers before turning yourself in?"

Dr. Swanson asked this as he finished writing. Dr. Horowitz was writing faster now. It seemed he wanted to finish his thought before David spoke again. David thought for a moment.

"I would have to guess it was several weeks. I was still incoherent for a day as my body processed the drugs still in my system. It took a great deal of time for me to build up the courage to allow others to see me. The media captured the rest of what happened after I surfaced."

Despite his roaring voice, David maintained a calm nature as he answered questions.

"Why did you go to the authorities before attempting to contact your loved ones?"

"My loved ones are still frightened of my appearance. I did not want to startle them, and I wanted people to know I was not dangerous. Or at least make them feel safe knowing I wasn't running free."

"So, you've accepted being a monster? Oh, I'm sorry, we don't like that word. You've accepted your change in appearance?"

Dr. Horowitz smirked as he interrupted Dr. Swanson. David shifted in his seat.

"I didn't want to alarm anyone. I knew people would react with anger toward my appearance."

David had raised his voice without realizing. Dr. Horowitz made him upset. Dr. Swanson regained control of the hearing.

"What was your relationship with them like before the incident?"

"What difference does it make what our relationship was like before when they can't stand to look at me now?"

The irritation David felt was becoming more prevalent. He felt anxiety and resentment towards his family for walking away when he needed them most. He also believed he was getting what he deserved. He believed this was all punishment for his past wrongdoings. He was ready to face the outside world having now accepted his fate and served his time in despair. It was time to heal.

Dr. Swanson documented several comments on his paper. Dr. Horowitz took this opportunity to take control.

"Tell us about your wife."

"Ex-wife, doctor. I signed the divorce papers she sent me last week." David took a deep breath after this statement.

"So, tell us about your ex-wife."

"She filed for divorce. What more do you need to know?"

"You don't seem upset about the divorce. Were there problems with the marriage?"

The tone in Dr. Horowitz's voice seemed almost antagonizing.

"My wife and I haven't spoken in months. My grief ended a long time ago. She only loved my looks; not who I was. The divorce was a relief."

"You don't seem relieved. Doesn't it make you angry? The thought of your wife being with another man because she can't stomach the sight of you; a hideous beast?"

"That's enough Dr. Horowitz!" Dr. Swanson said.

"It's all right. Your attempts to antagonize me are pointless, doctor." David said.

David was experiencing an emotional reaction to Dr. Horowitz's comments. He was trying to hold himself together. He grew tired of living like a prisoner in a mental health ward.

As Dr. Horowitz sneered at David, Dr. Swanson recommenced the hearing.

"You said your wife only loved your looks. Can you elaborate on that a little more?"

"I don't know if that's why she married me. It doesn't matter anymore."

David lowered his head as if everything that had happened had finally caught up and defeated him.

"Why are you avoiding the questions about your past?"

Dr. Quaid had finally broken his silence. David's irritation was now moving to anger.

"As I mentioned before, my past is irrelevant, doctor."

Dr. Horowitz's snide comments and Dr. Quaid seeming to not even listen had David feeling livid. Why was his future left into the hands of these men?

"I have no desire to remember it. I only wish to create a new future and that is why I agreed to attend this hearing."

Dr. Quaid leaned forward.

"Mr. Jones. If you believe your past is irrelevant, I fear you may detach yourself from the human condition."

David tried not to react to this statement, but he feared Dr. Quaid was right. He took a deep breath and clenched his clawed fists.

"There is much of my past I cannot remember especially from before the incident. The few memories I have are not pleasant ones. I do not want to be the person I remember."

David's claws were tearing into his trousers. His eyes were watering.

"If you don't have many memories, how do you know the ones you have are accurate? How do you know they depict who you were, Mr. Jones?"

Though he never met with David, Dr. Quaid was the supervising psychiatrist in charge of David's care. Anything involving his treatment needed approval from Dr. Quaid. Dr. Quaid had voiced his opinion against this hearing. He claimed David was not ready for reintroduction into society.

"I was a very selfish man. I showed concern only for myself and no one else, not even my wife. That's why I don't blame my family for leaving me. This is a punishment for all my wrongdoings."

David was fighting back tears as he spoke. His transformation was a humbling experience. Despite the misfortune it brought him, he was happy with whom he was becoming, even if he looked hideous.

"I have forgiven my family and want to grow from this experience."

Dr. Quaid had a surprised expression on his face as one of the security guards looked at the other.

"Is the beast crying?" The guard said.

David cleared his throat as the handsome doctor spoke again.

"Thank you, Mr. Jones. Please wait out in the hall and we will call you back in when we are ready."

David rose and walked back to the door with the security guards already opening it for him. The chair he was sitting in had bent from his weight. He stood outside the door as the doctors discussed his case. He wondered what they might be saying.

Dr. Swanson began their discussion. "All right gentlemen, should we allow Mr. Jones to reenter society? I say yes but only if he continues to meet with a therapist once a week."

"Are you joking!" Dr. Horowitz was as grumpy as ever. "Do you see what he did to that chair? Imagine what he can do to another person. He's still emotional and we don't even know how he would react to aggressive stimuli."

"He's been receiving aggressive stimuli since he revealed himself to the world. He hasn't harmed anyone in that entire time. He's managing any anger he has quite well."

"He's bottling up his emotions, Swanson. He's a time bomb waiting to explode, and he could kill someone and for all we know he'll eat them."

"That's nonsense, Doctor. He's shown no signs of cannibalism."

Dr. Horowitz laughed.

"He's not human so it would not be cannibalism. He's another species all together."

"Did he not convey human emotions? Tests show mutations in certain genes of his DNA. These mutations altered his appearance, but his mind is still human. He thinks and acts like a man. How would you feel if you were in his situation?"

"I would take my life for everyone else's safety!"

Dr. Horowitz and Dr. Swanson continued to argue as Dr. Quaid remained quiet. He remained undecided in his decision. It was difficult to think with those two crusty old men bickering like school children.

"He is not ready for the outside world." Dr. Quaid interrupted.

Dr. Horowitz seemed pleased with himself.

"He still has a long way to go, but I was unaware of how much progress he has made. I expected him to shout more and even throw his chair. I propose we keep him here for one more month at least."

"You would like to have another hearing one month from now?"

Dr. Quaid nodded at Dr. Swanson's question.

"What about you, Dr. Horowitz?"

Dr. Horowitz was almost snarling.

"I don't think he'll ever be fit to roam amongst the public, but we can reassess in a month."

"Then we're all agreed?"

Dr. Quaid nodded. Dr. Horowitz nodded with reluctance. Dr. Swanson walked over and typed a code on a keypad near the door. As he walked back to his seat, a buzzer sounded. The security guards opened the door and followed David back inside. David reclaimed his seat in the room's center. He hadn't noticed the chair's new deformity from his large body. He was more nervous than when he first entered the room. He did not feel confident about their decision.

"Mr. Jones, you have conducted yourself very well this afternoon."

Dr. Swanson cleared his throat. The security guards were still sweating from their silent encounter with David.

"You mentioned forgiving your family and accepting what has happened to you. These are paths towards positive growth, and you will continue to grow. But,"

David's heart raced. He knew this was coming.

"… we all feel releasing you would be a premature move. We would like to keep you here under observation for another thirty days. If you have continued showing consistent improvement, we will hold another hearing. Then we will determine how best to continue your treatment and get you back into the world. Do you have questions?"

David's mouth was dry. His eyes were watering again, but it was harder to hold them back. The guards stood at the ready expecting David to react with anger. He could only sob. He felt he was ready to start a new life. He only cried for a short duration before wiping his eyes and taking a deep breath.

"I have no questions. Thank you for the opportunity. I will work hard to better myself and become a contributing member of society. I look forward to showing you how much I will improve in the next few weeks."

Tears were still rolling down David's face as he spoke. Their decision upset him. He thought he might have a little farther to go before he could reclaim the life he lost so many months ago. Dr. Swanson told David he could leave. He made it back out into the hallway with the guards before he cried again. He turned to one guard.

"Yes, the beast can cry!"

They escorted him back down the long hallway to the elevator. It lifted them to the sixth floor with the only sound coming from the speakers in the elevator. David never spoke when escorted somewhere in the building. He knew breathing was enough to make the guards nervous. There were always different guards. David never saw someone more than once. He wondered if men were quitting, feeling they didn't get paid enough to fight a beast.

They walked down the sixth-floor hallway. It looked the same as the third-floor hallway except the numbers on the doors started with six. They stopped in front of room 627. The first guard unlocked the door. He opened it to reveal a small room with a bed, a sink and a toilet. There were white pants and a white shirt lying on the bed. On the pillow lay a book. These were the only belongings David owned.

He stepped into the room and the guards locked the door behind him. David heard one of them mumble something about the door not being big enough to hold him. It was possible but David never wanted to try. He feared his own strength and never wanted to use it. He changed into the white clothes and sat on his bed. It was still a while before dinner.

He had stopped crying on the way to his room but sobbed again. He felt defeated. He felt upset that he might never look human again. He was afraid they would treat him like a caged animal for the rest of his life. The tip of his tail lifted upwards and down as he sat on the bed; his crying subsided once again.

The only path he saw in front of him was to continue his treatment and hope he could leave after thirty days. He was ready for the discrimination he would face in the world, but he feared the world was not yet ready to face him.

Where the Bullfrogs Gather

A small mouse explored a patch of grass near a highway. A large bullfrog lurked behind him. The bullfrog yearned; waiting for the perfect moment. It closed its eyes and leaped into the air. The mouse continued exploring, unaware of the incoming attacker. Before landing, the bullfrog opened its mouth. Its tongue lurched out towards the mouse. The mouse disappeared with two quick bites. The bullfrog leaped away from the road as a Ford Granada raced down the highway.

The Granada ran to its limit; as fast as it could go; headlights splashing against the road and trees. Fear pushed the Granada to this speed; fear and urgency. The operator of the Granada looked to the back seat. There laid a woman making fast short breathes.

"Hold on honey. We'll be at the hospital soon."

"Ahhh! I am not having this baby in the car!"

"I'm going as fast as I can."

"It's not fast enough!"

"I'm already speeding, and this stretch of highway is dangerous at night."

"You're about to have danger in this backseat if we're not at the hospital soon!"

Something lurked across the tops of the trees as the Granada sped down the highway. It followed the car; waiting for the perfect moment. From within the trees, a dark figure leaped into the air, soaring through the moonlight. The Granada and those within continued down the highway, unaware of the attacker. With a loud thump, the figure landed on top of the car.

"What the hell was that!?"

"I don't know, keep breathing."

112

The driver looked up and then all around the car but couldn't see anything that caused the noise. The figure atop the car laid motionless. Another dark figure ran through the trees alongside the car. The driver didn't notice the figure in the darkness. The loud noise left the driver's mind as he focused on driving.

"Is something wrong with the car?"

"I don't think so. I'll check after I get you to the ER. We're almost back in town."

"How long?"

"Uh, ten minutes...?"

"Drive faster!"

The running figure threw something towards the car causing the rear tire to blow out. The driver fought to keep control of the Granada to stop it. The passenger atop the car vanished.

"I'll be right back. Shit. Shit!"

"Ahhh!"

"Shit."

The driver fumbled with the keys to open the trunk. He dropped to the ground to find a good place to lift the Granada. Three sets of legs waited in front of the car. The driver sprang up and waved a tire iron between him and the eyeless hooded corpses.

"Stay back!"

"What's going on Howard!? Can you change the...Ahhh...hurry!"

In an instant one creature stood next to the driver and snapped his neck.

"Howard? Howard! Answer me!"

The figure threw the pregnant woman from the car and snapped her neck. The three dark figures tore into the pregnant woman's stomach and fought over the unborn child.

Several minutes of flesh tearing and bone crunching occupied them.

"Nothing's happening."

"Should we have waited for birth?"

"Wait."

They fell thrashing. Their blood curdling screams echoed through the forest and down the highway. The screaming stopped. They laid motionless. Heavy breathing. Panting. Their hair changed from the frail, thin white to full, thick, shiny tresses. Skin and eyes formed. They climbed to their feet laughing.

"We're young again."

"Even younger than the last time we changed."

"How long's it been?"

"Too long."

"My skin is so smooth."

"How did you get red hair? I want red hair!"

"Well I want blonde hair. It would look great with my smooth skin."

"Quiet! We have so much to do. The world has changed. We must acclimate and blend in. Our youth won't last forever."

"I'd look better as a red head is all I'm saying."

"You both can change your hair when we get home. Or have you forgotten we can alter our appearances? Come."

"Why does she always have dark hair?"

"She never changes her hair. That's her natural color."

"So, I'm a natural blonde?"

"I don't remember. Are you?"

"We are plotting to kill those people who destroyed our families and all you two can talk about is hair color. Will you two focus, please?"

"Sorry."

"Yeah, sorry."

The three women returned to the darkness of the forest. Several bullfrogs searched for food. They waited for the insects to come for the carcasses. The Granada's headlights continued gazing on the road in silence.

Ceres

Ceres, a fast, little schooner, received her first commission in 1807 as a merchant ship. She began with a compliment of forty, including the Captain, Mates, and seamen. She made several trips across the Atlantic. The official manifests always listed her cargo as different types of food and drink. But on occasion she had humans restrained within her awaiting slavery. During the War of 1812, she transformed into a war ship. She only encountered two battles with British vessels. After considerable damage, she returned to the sea, rebuilt, as a merchant vessel.

Ten years after her commission, Ceres fell under the command of a privateer. Captain Edward Pike, called a privateer by his own country while others named him a pirate. The truth was he took any job that would pay whether legitimate or other. He experienced more horrors of the sea than most other captains. His skills would prove useful after finding an abandoned ship in the middle of the Caribbean Sea.

Captain Pike acted unusual compared to most captains. He chose a woman as his first officer, Ms. Maria Copeland. Years ago, some men fell prey to their primal urges with her on their ship.

"Step back or I'll remove your little tool you're so eager to use." She said.

"And I'll help her." The first mate said.

That first mate became Captain Pike. Several crewman and sailors received the same threats. Even after her commission, many men would not take orders from a woman. Those defiant sailors learned Ms. Copeland always followed through with her promised threats. The current crew respected her as much as the Captain. She gave her respect in return.

Captain Pike called Ms. Copeland to his chambers. Ceres approached the motionless vessel.

"Arrange a boarding party with two men from our crew and a couple of our passengers. Have them look for supplies." Captain Pike said.

"Aye, Sir. Mr. Burn and Mr. Gibbs have a good rapport with the passengers." She said.

"Thank you, Ms. Copeland. And if the passengers complain, remind them we allowed them on board at lower than standard pay." He said.

"Aye, Sir."

Maria Copeland, as tall as any man and twice as mean, spent many years earning her place on every ship she sailed. Captain Pike remained the only man to show her kindness. He saved her life on many sea voyages and she repaid the favor a few times. Mystery and secrecy surrounded the story of how Ms. Copeland and Captain Pike met.

"He pulled me out of the ocean many years ago."

Ms. Copeland never said more. She would never turn down an opportunity to tell anyone about a past adventure. But she never spoke about her life before meeting Captain Pike. Many would ask but the Captain would always give the same answer.

"Her life is her business and none of yours."

Most of their current crew sailed with them long enough to know not to pry into the past. They had heard many others try.

"Won't you tell us of the first adventure you and Ms. Copeland embarked on?"

"You're not to be fraternizing with the officers, boy."

"Mr. Burn. Mr. Gibbs. The Captain wants you to take a couple passengers and search the ship. See if anything is salvageable." Ms. Copeland said.

"Aye, Ma'am." Mr. Gibbs said.

117

"I know two passengers who will help. They're good men." Mr. Burn said.

Jimmy Gibbs sailed since he could climb onto a boat. He was the oldest member of the crew. As the ship's Boatswain and Quartermaster, he knew every inch of the boat and how best to operate it.

"Beggin' your pardon Captain but a bowline knot is best to tie this off."

"Very good, Mr. Gibbs. See that it's done."

"Aye, Sir."

Joseph Burn found freedom on the sea as a runaway slave. He always found work on ships as a skilled carpenter. Ship's carpenters often became surgeons since they had the necessary tools. But Mr. Burn worked for a surgeon in his youth and knew more than the average seaman. His race prevented him for ever going to medical school, but the surgeon taught him well.

"You may never be free Joseph, but you will be valuable to any man with these skills I've taught you. Do not waste them."

"Yes, Sir. I'll help people no matter their color."

"Good Lad."

The surgeon died, and his family sold Mr. Burn. He did not see kindness again until he met Captain Pike years later.

Several Freedmen from Florida traveled on the ship and Mr. Burn had befriended them. If he asked, he knew they would help search the abandoned ship.

"George. Peter. I'd like to ask a favor." Mr. Burn said.

"Whatever it is, we'll do it. You and your Captain helped us escape the war. We're forever in your debt." George said.

118

"We need help searching the abandoned ship. You don't mind?"

"Of course not. We owe you. I'd rather be dead than go back to that country." Peter said.

"They call it the United States but we're not all united." George said.

"On this ship we are all united." Mr. Burn said.

They followed simple orders. Search for the crew, search for food and water, and search for anything salvageable to use on the ship. If still intact, they could tow the ship back to port.

"I'll check the hold for supplies. I'll know better than you boys of what is salvageable. Peter, check the Captain's Cabin. George, check the Forecastle. Mr. Burn, with me." Mr. Gibbs said.

"Check the what?" George said.

"Crew quarters. Front of the ship. That door." Mr. Burn said.

"Savvy?" Mr. Gibbs said.

"Yes, Sir." George and Peter said.

Mr. Gibbs and Mr. Burn climbed down the hatch to the hold. Mr. Burn lit a lantern hanging next to the hatch ladder.

"What's that smell? Rotting flesh?" Mr. Burn said.

"All the barrels are empty. Another ship may have cleared it out." Mr. Gibbs said.

They walked towards the stern in the damp darkness. The smell grew stronger.

"There's your rotting flesh; human remains." Mr. Gibbs said.

Skeletons lay around the hold, but some still had flesh rotting away.

"See the chains. This was a slave ship. They must've starved to death. You think the crew abandoned the ship?" Mr. Burn said.

"Let's check the Captain's Log." Mr. Gibbs said.

"AHH!"

"That sounds like Peter." Mr. Burn said.

"What's going on!?" George said.

"Help me!"

Peter stumbled out holding his neck. He struggled to Ceres wet with crimson.

"What's going on!?" Ms. Copeland said.

"I don't know." Mr. Gibbs said.

The rest of the crew huddled around Peter.

"Were you attacked?"

Captain Pike pushed through the crowd to the bleeding man.

"What happened?"

"We don't know. We were below deck, Sir. He was in the Captain's Cabin." Mr. Burn said.

"Tell me who did this." Captain Pike said.

Peter struggled for words but only gasped for air. He fell, motionless as blood gurgled from his mouth.

"Ms. Copeland."

"Aye, Sir."

"Have the body prepared. Allow those who desire to pay their respects then release it to the ocean. No one boards the other ship until I say."

"Aye, Sir."

"Mr. Gibbs. Mr. Burn. Was anything found in the hold?"

"Only bodies, Sir." Mr. Gibbs said.

"Two from our crew and two from the passengers on watch all night. Make the arrangements, Mr. Gibbs."

"Aye, Sir."

Peter received a brief and solemn service. They tossed his body overboard as the Sun began to set.

"I heard a ghost killed him and that's why the old crew abandoned ship." One passenger said.

"No, he fell onto a broken board. I saw the gash in his neck." George said.

"He had bite marks on his neck."

"Oh, shut up, Sarah, you're always sayin' things that ain't true."

"It's true. I saw it. So, did she."

"I did."

"You're both pulling my leg." George said.

"Have all rifles and pistols loaded and all swords and knives sharpened before supper." Captain Pike said.

The passengers and crew grew anxious. Only Ms. Copeland and Captain Pike knew what evil lay ahead.

"How many do you expect to lose, Sir." Ms. Copeland said.

"Most of the passengers I suspect. We have a solid crew. They'll manage." Captain Pike said.

"How many do you think there are?"

"One or two. Three if Peter rises tonight."

"He will."

"I know. He won't understand what's happening. I doubt he'll remember dying. Wake me when it starts."

"Aye, Sir. I put your sword by the bedside."

"Thank you, Maria. Stay alive."

"I always do. I fought these things long before you found me."

Several uneventful hours passed. The night watchers took two-hour shifts. With so few crew members, even John the cook had a shift. John, a stocky short man with more hair on his arms than his head, held watch with Samuel Ford.

Samuel was a young boy with only a few months experience at sea.

"John. You see where them passengers on watch are?" Samuel said.

"They might've gone back to their bunks."

"I've come from the forecastle. They ain't there."

"The next watch starts soon. Let's wake 'em now and we'll all search the ship. Keep your head about you, boy."

"You think it some killer what make them go missing?"

"I don't know, but it don't feel right."

They woke the next passengers for watch, then Ms. Copeland and Ms. Flora Baker, the ship's main rigger.

"You sure have pretty hair Ms. Baker. You get it from yer mother or father?" Samuel said.

"That's a strange question this time of night. I get it from my mother. She was Cherokee. Never knew my father."

"How come?"

"He was a nameless soldier who beat and raped my mother."

"I'm sorry, Miss. I didn't know."

"Quit your flirtin', boy. You help the passengers search the ship. Ms. Baker, will you wake the rest of the crew? I'll speak to Ms. Copeland."

The ship creaked and swayed as they separated.

"Ma'am, some of the passengers are missing." John said.

Ms. Copeland nodded and yawned.

"I'll wake the Captain. Ready the weapons and get all the passengers in the hold. Be ready to fight"

"You know what's out there, Ma'am?"

"You'll know soon enough. Get everyone to the hold. I'll wake the Captain."

"Aye, Ma'am." John said.

Ms. Copeland knocked as she opened the Captain's door.

"You're awake? Um, its starting, Sir." She said.

"Thank you, Maria. I'll be out in a moment. It's all right Peter. She's gone. Come out from behind the curtains."

Peter, pale and perfused with sea water, emerged. His expression held both confusion and wonderment.

"What do you last remember, Peter?" Captain Pike said.

"I was searching the Captain's Cabin of the abandoned ship when it happened." Peter observed every item in the Captain Pike's cabin, as if seeing everything for the first time.

"I saw no one in the cabin. I first went to the desk piled with books. I saw the ship's manifest and ledger. This information did not make sense to me. I thought your quartermaster would find it interesting."

Peter's voice rang dream-like. He picked up a map of the Caribbean from Captain Pike's desk and examined it.

"I've seen many maps in my years including one of this region, but I swear this looks so new; different. Do you ever feel this way, Captain?"

"What happened after you found the ledger?" Captain Pike said.

"I found the Captain's Log. It was last dated only two weeks ago. A Captain Henry Smith threw his small crew overboard for mutiny. He wrote they tied him up and slaughtered the passengers and other human cargo. The last line said he would die without food.

"I then heard something moving in the closet. I thought it could be a rat. When I opened the door, there was nothing but old clothes. Decades old. I found this strange but turned to keep searching the room. Something grabbed me from behind and bit off a piece of my skin. I had never seen

123

so much blood. I held my neck, but it was too late. So much blood. I stumbled out and back to the ship. So much blood."

"Who bit you, Peter?"

"So much blood."

"Peter. Who bit you? Where is it now?"

"Then I saw you standing over me. I can hear your heart beat, Captain."

Captain Pike stood from his bed with his cutlass in hand. Peter, facing away from him, still looking over the contents of Captain Pike's desk.

"So much blood. In your heart."

With a blink of his eyes, Peter stood next to the Captain with his hand on the Captain's throat. Captain Pike thrust his cutlass into Peter's torso. Peter released the Captain and stepped back. He examined the new hole in his stomach with wonder and amusement.

"How strange this is. I don't even feel it." Peter said.

With a practiced and steady hand, Captain Pike cut off Peter's head with one swing. The wonder fell from his face as Peter's head rolled on the floor. Captain Pike took a deep breath and collected himself. He heard the screams from outside his cabin as he finished dressing.

"The past always comes back around." He said.

"CUT OFF THEIR HEADS!" Ms. Copeland said.

Captain Pike stepped out onto the deck as the carnage began.

"The dead are rising." Someone said.

"What are they?"

"VAMPIRES!" Ms. Copeland said.

Captain Pike never saw humans turned so fast into demons of the night.

"Stay back to back, men. We fight to the last." Ms. Copeland said.

"What of the Captain?"

"Do as he does!" Ms. Copeland said.

Ms. Copeland decapitated two creatures but dozens more waited on the other ship. An overzealous monster charged towards the Captain as he exited his cabin. Without breaking his stride, Captain Pike made one step to the right and pulled his right arm back. He stepped forward towards the creature, and with one punch knocked the creature down to the deck. He continued walking towards the other ship. The cabin boy Samuel ran over and decapitated the unconscious creature.

Captain Pike unsheathed his cutlass and drew his flintlock pistol. Two more monsters ran towards him. The first he shot in the face to slow it down. The second ran into his cutlass severing its head. Captain Pike flipped his pistol around grasping the barrel. The first creature pulled a sword and the Captain blocked it with his pistol. He pulled the sword down and cut off the first creature's head.

The crew followed the Captain to the other ship as the remaining monsters attacked. One remained motionless. Only the crew of the Ceres remained alive. The motionless creature viewed the bloodbath with a smile. He walked forward, and the other creatures stopped as he passed.

"Captain Pike, I presume." The creature said.

"Who are you?"

"Captain Henry Smith. We've never met but I'm familiar with your work with the mermaids. You live up to your reputation."

"What do you want, vampire?" Captain Pike said.

"Food for us is hard to come by at sea. What we find we must ration. My former crew gave in to their cravings and depleted our reserves. I killed them all. I wish to offer you a proposition. You all fight well. You're strong. I'll spare your lives if you agree to man our ship during the day while we sleep. You will also help me keep those I've turned in line."

"If you know me so well, then you know I'll never agree to those terms. I don't work for Hell spawns." Captain Pike said.

"Either you agree, or you die. You have no mermaids to help you now."

"Wrong!" Ms. Copeland said.

"It is you Grizelda. I almost didn't recognize you. Ha, what have you done to yourself?"

"I don't remember you." She said.

"I'm hurt, my dear. Do you remember my former name? Grimwald."

Captain Pike and Ms. Copeland traded looks, faces white and pale. The other vampires laughed.

"What will it be, Captain?" Grimwald said.

"Are the barrels in place, Mr. Gibbs?" Captain Pike said.

"Aye, Captain."

"The answer is still no, Monster! NOW!"

Mr. Gibbs fired a pistol at a barrel nearest the vampires. Filled with gunpowder, it exploded. Other barrels nearby exploded from the chain reaction setting both ships on fire. The crew jumped off the ship and gathered on life boats stocked with supplies for a long voyage. The explosions distracted the vampires from stopping the crew. Grimwald shouted over the roaring flames.

"I will have my vengeance, Grizelda. I will have the heads from your family!"

The crew rowed off in two life boats. They had many questions for the Captain and Ms. Copeland, but none could muster the courage to ask. They all stared at the raging inferno. Their home would soon fall into the sea.

"She was a grand ship." Mr. Gibbs said.

"Aye." John said.

"No other ship be like her." Samuel said.

126

"You only been on the one ship." Mr. Burn said.

"And I'll remember her forever. She was our home."

"We'll get a new ship. Home is here on these boats. Every one of us. Even with all the secrets, we'll have a home as long as we're together."

"Well said, Ms. Baker." Captain Pike said.

The other ship sank into the sea before Ceres. She had no chance of defeating the fire, but she held on as long as she could. Her final purpose; saving her crew, an honorable mission. She carried the vampires; those monsters, to their deaths. Grimwald made an escape on a piece of driftwood; one he could hide under during the day. The other creatures died in the flames as Ceres fell underneath the care of the sea.

Of the many captains who commanded her in her adventurous life, Captain Pike took the most care. The Crew planned to build Ceres anew. Aided by Ms. Copeland's former family, Ceres would rise from the ashes.

The Fall of the Foot

The alley seemed to shrink the harder the rain poured. The street lights broke the darkness of the night. Clotheslines stretched across buildings, tied to fire escapes. One shirt was still hanging, defiant of the rain.

Yoshi splashed through puddles. He maneuvered around piles of trash as he ran faster with only sandals between the ground and his feet. Yoshi was being chased. A rat steadied itself atop his shoulder clutching for dear life. Yoshi looked back to see if anyone followed him. At first, he saw no one, then from the shadows a figure charged after him. The attacker wore a hooded mask that covered everything but his eyes.

Yoshi looked back again as he ran into the street. He did not notice the truck coming towards him. The driver slammed on the brakes swerving on the wet road. The truck crashed, breaking store windows. It wedged between the buildings and a fire hydrant spraying water mixing with the hard rain. One barrel the truck carried rolled onto the road. A green slimy substance spread from it like lava from a volcano.

Yoshi lay in the road lifeless as his attacker approached. The masked man removed a small dagger from his belt and pressed it into Yoshi's chest. The rat from Yoshi's shoulder, covered in the slimy substance, sprang forth. The attacker peeled the rat from his face leaving one deep gouge down his right eye as he threw the rodent. He removed his dagger and ran off covering his eye.

The rat lay in the slimy substance, motionless but still alive. Four small turtles had fallen from the broken pet store window. Two were crawling towards the rat while one was wandering towards Yoshi's body. One other turtle was still on his back trying to turn over as the substance moved around him. The first turtle to reach the rat nudged him with his nose.

Leonardo
Thursday, July 18th

Leonardo woke to the sound of large trucks blasting down the roads outside. He had taken shelter in an abandoned house. The early morning sunlight beamed through the cracks of the boarded windows. He had lived in hiding all his life; no one reacted well to seeing a large talking turtle. With dark green, scaly skin, a heavy dark shell covering his back, he stood five foot six inches. People rarely responded well to his appearance, but Leonardo never got used to living on his own.

It was three years since he last saw any of his brothers. This was around the same time they all lost their surrogate father. Their Ninjitsu Sensei, Master Splinter; a large mutated, dark-haired rat. Oroku Saki, the leader of the Foot Clan sent his minions to assassinate Master Splinter. Oroku Saki had murdered Master Splinter's owner, Yoshi, beginning their lifelong feud. One of Leonardo's brothers, Donatello, went to confront the murderers. He never returned. Fearing the worst, Leonardo went to search for him. His other two brothers had argued against it. Leonardo was still searching.

The Foot Clan had taken control of Manhattan Island five years ago. In that time, they seized the entire state of New York and were taking the rest of New England. Many within and out of the clan knew their leader as the Shredder. His small group of followers helped brainwash young teenagers. They turned them into loyal soldiers for his cause. As the teenagers grew both in age and skill, The Foot defeated and held back the United States Military. They continued to take control, always increasing their numbers.

Their master trained Leonardo and his brothers to fight and stop The Foot but what could they do now? Separated for so long, Leonardo was not sure if they were still alive. He could only continue searching for them; always moving, never staying in one place for long. He could handle small groups, but The Foot always outnumbered him. His primary mission was to remain in the shadows until he found his brothers. Then they could avenge their master's murder.

There were more soldiers than usual that morning. He was not sure what was happening, but Leonardo knew it had nothing to do with him. The soldiers prepared for a large attack as Leonardo looked outside. While he felt lucky, he knew it was time to move before anyone discovered him. He donned a rubber mask which gave him a human face, and an overcoat to cover his unique body. He grabbed a large stuffed satchel and a long cylinder case. He opened the case to make sure he still had his Katana sword. The satchel contained food rations and water. It also held the pieces of another Katana sword, which broke in a fight a year before. He strapped the case with the katana under his arm, concealed by the overcoat. He threw the satchel over his neck. It was time to leave unseen.

It was safer to move at night, but Leonardo had to take the risk with how many soldiers were roaming about. After living on the run for so long, he would often get sick in confined places. He always watched the doors and windows. He planned many escape routes, contingency plans and more contingencies. He only got a couple hours sleep each night. Paranoia was an understatement. After losing his family and the Foot hunting him for so long, Leonardo trusted no one. He would not allow himself to be in a vulnerable position. Relaxation had become a faded memory.

Ten minutes had passed and there was no sign of any soldiers. He stayed close to the buildings as he hurried down the street in case he needed to find a quick hiding place. He felt a strong force push him from behind propelling him a few feet forward. His fall had knocked the wind out of him. His ears were ringing as he tried to catch his breath. He stood up and saw dozens of people running from the building that had exploded behind him. He saw they were shouting but did not know what. He only heard ringing. One man ran up to him and pointed his rifle at Leonardo. He was shouting but Leonardo did not understand. The man raised the butt of his rifle and hit Leonardo in the face. The ringing continued and his vision blurred. Leonardo felt another blow to the head, the ringing stopped, and everything went black.

***

"Hey Raph! Come here." Leonardo said.

"I'm Mikey!"

Leonardo shrugged.

"Sorry. You all look alike."

The four brothers were still young and looked similar. They were all over five feet tall. The only one who could ever tell them apart was Master Splinter.

"If you see who you all are on the inside and do not look at what is on the outside, you will know your brothers and yourself." Their master said.

He recognized their individual personalities. Donatello's intelligence. Michelangelo's free spirit. Raphael's sarcasm. Leonardo's leadership. But this was something the brothers did not understand. Raphael chimed into the conversation.

"You look the same as us."

"Well, we should try wearing different color bandanas instead of all wearing red?" Donatello said.

"I like the red! I ain't changin!" Raphael said.

Avoiding another argument, Leonardo conceded.

131

"Fine, you can keep red. Donnie, do we have any other bandanas?"

"I'm sure I can find some."

***

Leonardo could hear muffled voices. He tried to look for who was speaking but his vision was blurry, and the voices sounded far away. He sat up from the bed and held his head. He had never had a headache this severe. The voices sounded clearer and less distant.

"It's waking up. What should we do with it?" A man said.

"We need to find out why they made it. Let's hope it speaks."

Leonardo looked up. His vision focused and he realized he was in a jail cell with a man and woman standing on the other side of the bars. They had taken his weapon, mask, and satchel. He only had his blue bandana.

The woman spoke to him first. She looked petite but strong. Covered with Kevlar and a rifle slung on her shoulder, she looked like she could hold her own in a fight. Leonardo noticed she also had a pistol strapped to her right thigh.

There was strength in her voice.

"Why did they create you? Was it to destroy the resistance?"

"Coffee."

"What?"

His response surprised the woman.

"If you want to know about me, get me a cup of coffee and some aspirin. My head is killing me."

He was groggy, and this made Leonardo wonder how many hours he had slept. There were no windows in his cell. How long had they been holding him? Who were they?

The woman waited a moment looking him over.

132

"Keep an eye on him."

She left the room. Leonardo heard her talking to someone outside the door. He could not make out what they were saying. He focused his attention on the stern-looking man staring at him. He was forcing his face to look angry. A trick Leonardo had used when interrogating others. Leonardo did not feel the man was very scary.

Leonardo surveyed him. He was holding a rifle with a pistol on his hip. He wore a ballistic chest plate, a knife in his boot or a smaller pistol. His pockets were full of what Leonardo thought were magazines for the rifle.

His head still hurt but not as bad as when he woke. Now that things were clearer, he reviewed his surroundings. He was sitting on a cot in a small cage. Leonardo thought they had converted the room to hold prisoners. He assumed they had converted an office building into their hideout. The room was a little bigger than the cage with only one door. There was no place for him to go to the bathroom which made him sure the cage was a temporary holding.

"What do I have to do to use the bathroom?" He said.

The guard did not reply but continued glaring at Leonardo.

He must think he's intimidating. Leonardo thought.

The woman returned with a cup of coffee. She set it on the ground outside the cage then stepped back against the wall with the guard. Leonardo waited a moment before picking up the small cup. He inspected it; sniffed it. He felt the steam on his face and could smell the warm aroma of the darkness that would soon pour down his throat. It was enticing. He took a sip, burning his tongue a little as he savored the bitter, bland taste. He couldn't remember the last time he had coffee.

"Did he say anything?" The woman said.

"He wants a bathroom." The guard said.

133

"You won't be here long enough to worry about that." She said.

"Then you might as well kill me now." Leonardo said.

He was ready for his last fight though he did not want to die. Dying meant allowing one's self to become vulnerable. This seemed to startle his captures.

"We want to know what The Foot is planning, and you will tell us. We have ways of making you talk."

Leonardo thought this was a cliché comment. She was sure of herself. Leonardo suspected she forced her way into leadership with that same intimidation. It did not work on him.

"Even if I was part of The Foot, I wouldn't tell you a damn thing."

His voice still croaky, Leonardo sipped his steaming coffee.

An alarm blared from outside the room. Leonardo held his head in pain.

The woman ran out of the room muttering.

"I bet that's his friends coming to rescue him."

Leonardo chuckled.

"I have no friends."

He stood up and walked to the gate of the cage, staring back at the guard. He took another sip of the coffee than held it for a moment. The alarm was a bonus, but the rest of his plan was working to perfection.

He threw the hot coffee into the guard's face. He screamed and stumbled toward the cage, holding his face. Leonardo grabbed his chest plate and slammed his head against the cage, knocking him out. He pulled the keys off the guard's belt and opened the cage. The alarm had muffled the guard's scream. No one ran in the room to his aide.

Leonardo put his ear against the door. He only heard the alarm.

He cracked the door. No one was outside the room. He stepped out and saw his gear in the corner.

These people don't know what the hell they're doing. He thought.

He never secured a prisoner's weapon anywhere near where he held prisoners in case they escaped. Then they would spend their time searching for weapons instead of escaping.

He moved through the halls to find the exit. No one was around. He thought everyone was responding to the alarm. He found the stairs and ran up two flights to the ground level. He could hear the gunfire getting louder.

He saw several men and women fighting an advancement of Foot soldiers. The Foot outnumbered them, and they would not survive. Leonardo hesitated for a moment. Survival told him to leave, to run; like he had done so many times before. The rebels were not great fighters. No one else would help them.

Several soldiers broke through the small rebel force's barrier. Leonardo flew out the door unsheathing his Katana sword. The rebels were retreating to the building as he ran. Despite having rifles, The Foot soldiers were no match for Leonardo's skills with a blade. One by one, he would cut their weapons out of their hands and then either slice their chest open or behead them. Leonardo's movements were so quick, they only heard screams and saw blood splatter. It was a horrifying sight. Some rebels were barricading the building in case this monster came for them.

In his younger years, Leonardo never would have killed anyone. Living through constant Hell and being alone for so long had changed his way of thinking. He was a killer now and carried that guilt with both pride and sadness. Proud of winning the fight but sad for the terror he had caused. How many families were now fatherless or motherless because of his destruction? The thought would drive Leonardo crazy if he continued allowing it to fester in his mind.

The Foot retreated when they saw Leonardo in the fight. The rebels were still in shock. The woman who had attempted to interrogate Leonardo was awestruck. Leonardo thought they might want him to train them. He did not want to be around people for that long. He hoped they would be too afraid of him to ask.

He walked up to the woman.

"We need to get these people out of here. They'll be back and they'll cause more damage than you can imagine getting rid of me."

"Who… what are you?"

"I'm a giant turtle trained in the art of Ninjitsu and I've been fighting The Foot since before I can remember. Now do as I say, and you might stay alive."

"Do you have a name?"

Leonardo was getting agitated by the woman's questioning.

"Call me Leo."

"I'm Cynthia. Thank… thanks for the help."

Leo marched back into the building as Cynthia followed and the other rebels moved out of his way. He still needed to use a bathroom.

Michelangelo
Tuesday, July 16th

He had converted the small room into a dojo. Weapons hung all along the walls. Today Michelangelo was practicing with his favorite, the Nunchaku. Two sticks connected by a short chain or rope better known as nun-chucks. He had spent several years mastering many weapons. But these were the first weapon he mastered. He always felt more comfortable with nun-chucks.

The sessions in his small dojo were getting longer and harder. He was training for something, pushing himself harder than ever before. In his youth, he was a carefree and easygoing soul; always the first to come up with a joke. He didn't tell jokes anymore.

He stopped for a moment to drink water. There was a pounding coming from the door. Irritation grew in his face.

"Sorry Sir, I know you didn't want to be disturbed."

"What do you want?"

"Jones and O'Neil have returned."

"Thank you, I'll be out in a moment."

It was time to test his training. Six months passed since he saw them, Casey Jones and April O'Neil. Michelangelo had sent them out to recruit and gain intelligence on the Foot. They were always trying to expand their territory. He needed to know the weakest points of their stronghold. He needed someone with knowledge of the inside.

Michelangelo had spent the last five years building an army to rival the Foot. In the beginning he only trained new fighters. Jones and O'Neil were the first. Lately he had spent more time organizing tactical field operations against the Foot. He couldn't remember the last time he smiled.

After putting all the weapons away, he made his way out to the main hangar. The bunker was a few miles underground. Abandoned after the Cold War, he made it his base of operations. He could hear the elevator descending as he approached the end of the hangar. The freight elevator came to a stop and two guards opened the gate door. Jones and O'Neil exited with about twenty-five other men and women. Jones was easy to spot. He still wore a hockey mask.

In all the years Michelangelo had known him he always wore the mask, more so to hide his face than to guard it. Michelangelo almost didn't recognize O'Neil. Her age was showing; a few wrinkles, coarse hair, and eyes that showed strength and wisdom. He knew she was more capable of taking out enemies than any of the men. Michelangelo could see that Jones knew it too but would never admit someone was better than him.

Jones's muffled voice echoed through the hanger.

"Mese arr all wee cold gen."

"Take the damn mask off, Jones." Michelangelo said.

"He said this is all we could get. We had more but some of them didn't make it." O'Neil said.

"I still want him to take the mask off. The Foot wear masks, we don't! Many years ago, I had a Foot assassin disguise himself with a hockey mask and try to kill me. No Masks!"

Michelangelo was serious about this. He never wore his orange mask anymore. No one understood why. He never shared how a Foot assassin disguised himself as Casey Jones. The assassin captured Master Splinter and later killed him. Michelangelo never forgave himself for that mistake. This gave him more drive than anything else in his life.

Jones removed his mask.

"Come on, Mikey. It's not that big of a deal."

"Yes, it is. I want to see everyone's face, especially if they're in my bunker."

He stepped closer to Jones and almost whispered, "And don't call me Mikey in front of the other soldiers."

Jones nodded.

Mikey had gotten good at remembering faces. He had hundreds of recruits and could remember each and everyone's face. He could never remember a name unless he saw them every day.

138

Mikey trusted Jones and O'Neil more than anyone else. But over the last year his trust in anyone was fading. He was coordinating a plan to infiltrate the Foot's stronghold. Only certain people knew certain parts of the plan. He never shared all the details with anyone.

Despite any paranoia Mikey may have had, he made sure not to let anyone see it. He wouldn't allow anyone to question his leadership.

"Get these people fed and rested. Their training starts tomorrow."

"Some of them already have training, Mikey."

Jones always had trouble staying quiet.

"They haven't had my training. The chow hall is to your right."

Mikey went upstairs to his private office.

"I'll eat in my office."

"Yes Sir. I'll have it sent up."

He heard the guard order his food over the radio as he closed the door. It was not unusual for him to eat in his office. His cluttered desk held several aerial photos of the Foot's base. Getting them had not been easy. He lost a helicopter and four soldiers. One, the copilot, died before they returned to develop the film. His plan would never work unless he could find a weak point in the Foot's stronghold. So far, there was no simple way to get inside.

They attempted to break in many times, but all had failed. The Foot continued building more and more walls around the perimeter of their base. There were now twelve full walls surrounding the main base. A thirteenth was under construction. They spaced their walls one mile apart from each other. The closer the wall was to the primary base; the more soldiers were guarding it. They constructed the walls within the last two or three years. They continued advancing their area of control.

No one had seen the Shredder, leader of the Foot, since they built the second wall. It was not long after that Mikey stopped trusting anyone when they took Master Splinter. He gazed at a photo on his wall of his brothers. Leonardo, Raphael, Donatello, and himself with Jones, O'Neil and Master Splinter. They took it only a few months before the war started.

"Those were happier times." He said.

***

"Come on, Mikey!" April said.

"Yeah, hurry and set the camera timer."

Donatello sat on the floor next to Master Splinter and Raphael.

"You're gonna miss the picture."

Leonardo stood behind Master Splinter with Casey next to him.

"Okay, okay it's ready. Everyone say, 'Ninja Pizza!'"

Michelangelo ran over to everyone else and stood next to April with Raphael in front of him. They all shouted as the camera flashed.

"NINJA PIZZA!"

***

There was a knock at the door. It was loud and quick, almost startling him.

"Come in."

O'Neil walked in with a plate of food.

"I brought you dinner. Everything okay?"

"Thank you. I'm working out details of the Foot's base. They have been very thorough."

"I wanted to talk to you about something in private if that's all right."

She looked worried. She never worried.

"What is it? Did something happen?"

"Something, well, strange."

140

"How strange? I don't like strange."

"You used to. On our way back today, a patrol a few miles west of the Foot base hit us. They seemed surprised to find us. They immediately opened fire. They outnumbered us so we ran and prayed. We lost many people, but we made it. What's strange is someone, some lone fighter, distracted them so we could escape. The patrol was searching for him when they found us. He was fast. Faster than you. All I could see was a blur and Foot soldiers dropping left and right. He took out the whole patrol by himself. One of the Foot soldiers came running behind us; running from him not after us. This guy, wearing an overcoat and a cloth around his face, threw something. I didn't know what, and it took down the soldier. We kept running, but I looked back one more time and saw him, whoever he was, reclaim his weapon. He carried a pair of Sais, with the three prongs like Raphael's. He looked at me, nodded, and ran off into the shadows."

Mikey smiled a hopeful smile.

"I don't think it's strange. Have you told anyone else?"

"Only Jones."

"Who's he told?"

His expression went from hopeful to stern.

"I told him not to tell anyone."

Mikey gave her a look she knew meant he did not believe her.

"Believe it or not, he listens about important things like this. He thinks the same thing I do, about who that guy might be."

"And who do you think it is? Raphael?"

She looked at the photos on his desk, raised her eyebrows and looked back at him.

141

"Whoever he is, we need to find him. He might know what we need to break through the Foot's defenses. One more thing,"

O'Neil was about to leave.

"We brought back tomatoes, so I asked the chef to make us a pizza for later."

Mikey smiled.

"I haven't had pizza in years."

Raphael
Tuesday, July 16ᵗʰ

Fifty soldiers surrounded him. That might seem overwhelming to some, but for Raphael it was a descent workout. Most of them were still young and didn't know how to fight. It would take years of training for any of the soldiers to come close to being a match for him. Or his weapon of choice; a pair of Sai which look like miniature tridents.

He studied the art of Ninjitsu since he was young. Ever since the accident that changed him from a regular turtle. The accident that changed Raphael and his brothers, and their surrogate father. It changed them into mutated creatures.

For many years Raphael hated what he was. He always wanted to walk the streets of New York without fear and without frightening others. Now there was nothing but fear in the streets of what used to be New York. Soldiers fell left and right as he defeated them with ease.

The Foot is training them better but they're still no match for me. He thought.

He defeated them without breaking a sweat. The Foot usually sent out patrols to find Raphael. This time he found them attacking a group of rebel soldiers. He wore several layers of clothes to hide the enormous shell on his back and to cover his green skin. Most of the rebels were busy running but Raphael spent a moment looking at one. She looked like someone he used to know years ago but he was not sure. He hoped it was someone he knew.

If that's April, then that means Mikey is still fighting. He thought.

It was a long time since Raphael had seen his brother, Mikey. He left his brothers shortly after Master Splinter died.

***

"How could you let this happen?" Raphael said.

"I thought… I thought it was Casey. He knocked me out. I didn't know, Raph."

Michelangelo was fighting back tears as he looked at his Master's lifeless body on the floor.

"I didn't know."

"That's why we always tell you to pay attention! You never pay attention and now Master Splinter is dead! You killed him!"

"It's not his fault Raph and you know it."

Leonardo stepped between his brothers as Donatello sobbed behind him.

"And where the Hell were you!? Some leader you turned out to be. I'm outta here."

"Raph, wait!" Michelangelo said.

"Let him go. He'll come back when he calms down."

Leonardo picked up a blanket and cover Master Splinter's body. He kneeled down by the head of his former father figure, wiping tears from his eyes.

***

It took several weeks for Raphael's anger to subside. He felt terrible for what he had said to his brothers. He made a promise to avenge Master Splinter's death and took a vow of silence. He believed he would never see his brothers again but always searched for them. None of them lived in the

143

home they shared with Master Splinter anymore. Raphael always feared his brothers had died.

After helping the rebel soldiers, he felt hope that one of his brothers was alive. Raphael began the long walk back to his newest home. It was a small village far from the city where some refugees had taken shelter. Though he never spoke to them, the villagers always accepted him and brought him food. He always looked forward to walking back home.

Raphael walked for several hours. It would be dark soon, but he didn't worry. He enjoyed walking, especially in the evening. He was far enough away from areas the Foot controlled so he could take his time and walk in peace. Despite the half-destroyed buildings, Raphael always enjoyed the sunsets. He would gaze at the pink, purple, and orange clouds in the sky as the sun disappeared into the horizon. He would often wonder why he never appreciated the sunset before.

Still gazing at the sunset, he arrived in the small camp where he lived the last couple years. There were small groups of families that had come together to form a small community of refugees. They lived in peace, far enough away from the fighting, and that is why Raphael continued to stay with them. He would go out every couple of days to help the fighting rebels. He made sure no one followed him so the Foot would never find his sanctuary.

He always kept his disguise on so no one would come looking for him. The Foot would notice if people are talking about giant turtles. He always kept to himself and since he never spoke, few people ever tried to talk to him.

He always wondered what they thought of him.

They must think I'm strange for sleeping on the ground outside.

If they thought he was strange, they never showed it. Sometimes small children would bring him food and ask for fighting lessons. There was not much he could teach them without speaking but they would mimic his movements. He never showed them how to use weapons.

He would overhear rumors of a giant turtle inside the Foot's main base killing soldiers with a Katana sword.

I don't know how true they are, but I hope Leonardo is still alive.

He knew Donatello was missing for many years and believed he was dead like Master Splinter. He wondered if he should try to find Michelangelo.

I miss my brothers.

Wednesday, July 17th

Raphael spent most of the day resting and meditating. The children were never far away watching him. Some even imitated him as he meditated.

I strengthen my mind while they try to understand what it is I do.

One mother would always come to collect them.

"Leave him be." She said.

Giving Raphael a half a smile as if she were helping him get rid of some nuisance. He never minded the children.

Is that how I was with Master Splinter?

It was almost Raphael's favorite time of day, sunset, when one child ran to him to say there were soldiers coming. Raphael recognized them as the same group he had helped the day before. He listened to them speak to the mother who always told the children to leave him alone.

"We want to speak with that man."

One soldier pointed to Raphael. The woman looked confused.

"But he doesn't speak; to anyone. He never has."

A female soldier walked over to him.

She looks like April. If she is then the man next to her must be Casey.

"Are you Raphael?" She said.

He nodded.

The refugees gasped.

One child said, "There are giant turtles!"

Michelangelo emerged from the crowd. Raphael removed the cloth covering his face. More people gasped.

"You stopped speaking?" Michelangelo said.

Raphael nodded.

"Since Master Splinter?"

Raphael looked down and after a moment nodded again.

"Look, Raph... I..."

Raphael held his hand up to stop him. Raphael hugged him, fighting back tears. Michelangelo was also trying to stop himself from crying.

I hope that showed him I forgive him.

April threw her arms around Raphael.

"It's good to see you again."

Casey followed but only offered a handshake. Raphael hugged him. He seemed uncomfortable but Raphael understood.

I used to be like him. He thought.

Michelangelo got straight to business.

"We need a way into the Foot's stronghold. Can you help us?"

Raphael nodded.

"We can leave in the morning. May we stay here for the night?"

He nodded again.

"It will take a little getting used to. You not speaking."

Raphael smiled and nodded again.

146

Michelangelo spent many hours telling Raphael everything that had happened to him. Raphael could not stop himself and smiled the entire time. He felt a sense of pride for his little brother.

He has finally grown up.

"Have you heard the rumors of Leo inside their stronghold?" Michelangelo said.

Raphael nodded.

"Do you know anything about Donnie?"

Raphael sighed and shook his head.

They were both silent for a moment. They feared the worst. Michelangelo finally broke the silence.

"Well, we have an important day tomorrow. Better get to sleep. I'm glad to have you back, Raphael."

He smiled and gave Michelangelo another hug. He remained sitting by the fire alone, feeling happier than he had in many years.

It's good to have you back, little brother. He thought.

Reunion
Thursday, July 18th

"Are you sure this thing will fight alongside us?"

Some other rebels nodded as one of them pointed toward Leonardo.

"You saw how the Foot ran from him. We need him."

Cynthia may have been hesitant at first, but something made her trust the giant mutant turtle.

"But can we trust him?" The man said.

"No!"

Leo emerged from the bathroom.

"If you're smart you won't trust anyone, not even each other. They'll be coming back soon with more fighters. We need to move."

One rebel was furious.

"Who made you boss?"

There was an explosion on the wall close to them. Leo ran out looking for the Foot. He only saw rebel soldiers charging through, but he maintained his fighting stance. The soldiers stopped in front of him.

"We have another one!" One soldier said.

Leo thought his eyes played tricks on him. Walking through the rubble towards him were four familiar faces he had not seen in years. April O'Neil, Casey Jones, and his brothers Michelangelo and Raphael.

Without thinking, he threw his sword up and shifted his eyes fast between the four of them. He remembered the nightmares of the Foot Clan, disguised as his brothers, trying to kill him.

They won't trick me this time.

"Leo! It's us!"

Mikey was slow to approach him, hands up, as the others stopped.

"Stop right there!" Leo said.

Mikey did not move.

"Tell me something only Mikey would know."

Leo was suspicious. He kept his sword up, inches from Mikey's face.

Mikey thought for a moment.

"When we were ten, we were first learning how to fight with weapons. You guys used to make fun of me because I would always hit myself in the head. I always thought you guys hated me or that I let you down. So, I practiced until I was good. And then I let Master Splinter die… I let you guys down."

Mikey stood firm as tears rolled down his face. Raphael walked up behind Mikey and hugged him. Leo stood still for a moment, his sword now by his side. There were no tears, but everyone could see the pain in his face. Before Leo could speak, someone shouted.

"Contact Front! Three hundred meters!"

The Foot returned with more men.

"Bring in the Tank!" Mikey said.

The Foot retreated as the tank burst through the wall and fired on them. Mikey continued with commands.

"The tank is on point. You men follow along and use it as cover. Everyone else stay fifty meters behind!"

He looked at Leo.

"We need to get to the center of the base; can you take us there?"

Before he could answer, Cynthia jumped up.

"I can!"

"Can your men fight?" Mikey said.

"We've been doing this for a couple years now."

"Good, bring them with us. You stay with me."

"I never saw you as the leading type, Mikey." Leo said.

"And I never thought of Raph as the silent type." Mikey said.

Leo looked at Raphael.

"What's he talkin about?"

Raphael smiled and hugged him, then continued walking. Leo stood bewildered for a moment, then sheathed his sword and moved on with the others.

The Rebels and Turtles pressed on for over an hour. They broke down walls, took out snipers, avoided land mines and grenades. More and more soldiers loyal to the Foot Clan seemed to crawl from the ground and out of the walls. Bodies piled up with every wall they pushed through. When the rebels used up their ammunition, they grabbed anything on the ground. The closer they got to the Foot Clan Headquarters the harder it took to get through. They only had one wall left to breach and there seemed to be no one around protecting it.

Leonardo got nervous.

"This is too easy. Where is everybody?"

"There's electromagnetic shielding around the bunker. It protects them from aerial attacks and kills anyone who tries to get in."

Mikey pulled out a flashlight and blinked it.

"I have someone inside who can disable it so we can get in and find the Shredder."

"Do you trust this inside man?" Leo said.

"No."

A blinking light appeared on top of the bunker. The source of the blinking light shut down the electrical coil that powered the shield. They moved inside the wall and found several of the Foot standing guard. The fight was brutal, with bodies and blood falling everywhere. One man almost took off Leo's head, but Casey intervened.

"Get inside! We'll hold these guys."

Leo, Mikey and Raphael ran into the compound. It looked deserted. There was a single room with stairs leading upwards. Computers and wires littered the whole place. There was a rotting corpse near them with several smashed electronics around it.

A voice echoed through the room.

"There he is, the mighty Shredder. Well, he hasn't been mighty for some time."

"Who's there?" Mikey said.

"Well, that's rude! You don't recognize my voice?"

Leo's eyes were shifting around the room. He only saw two exits but couldn't find the source of the voice.

"Is this your man inside, Mikey?"

"Oh, no! You haven't heard from me in some time." The voice said.

"I don't like this." Mikey said.

"Michelangelo, why are you so serious?"

The voice grew louder.

"Tell me a joke."

"Who are you?" Mikey said.

"That wasn't funny."

The source of the voice burst out from behind the computer screens. Monitors, wires, and plastic debris littered the floor. It was Donatello charging after them. Their own brother, with maniacal rage painted on his face. He leaped onto Michelangelo, knocking him on his back, shouting.

"THAT... WASN'T... FUNNY... THAT... WASN'T... FUNNY!"

Donatello picked him up and slamming him down with every word. Leo tackled him off Mikey. They began fighting and Raphael went to Leo's aid.

Once Mikey caught his breath, he tried to stop them.

"Donnie, what are you doing?"

Donatello's movements were wild and savage. He attacked each of his brothers like a vicious animal.

"Donnie, we want to help you! What should we do?" Leo said.

"DIE!" Donnie said.

The three were overwhelming him. Donnie backed into a corner with fear set in his eyes. He laughed.

"You won't win."

With a menacing smile, Donnie grabbed Raphael's hand. He shoved the Sai threw his own face, killing himself. He fell to the floor, twitching.

"NO!!"

Leo fell to his knees and held the still twitching body. Raphael and Mikey were motionless; stupefied.

"What... what happened to you, Donnie?" Leo said.

"They captured him many years ago." A voice said.

"The Shredder brainwashed him. He hoped to use your brother against you, but he grew too strong to control. He killed the Shredder and took control of the Foot."

An old man stood at the end of the stairs.

"The Shredder's experiments drove him mad. It destroyed his mind. I am sorry, but today the Foot dies with him."

"Who are you?" Mikey said.

"I'm the one who helped you get inside." The old man said.

"I once stood at the Shredder's side. When your brother took control, he made us do unspeakable things. We had to stop him."

Leo still sobbing, pulled out the Sai from Donnie's face, picked up his body and carried it outside. The fighting had stopped. Few were still alive. The old man had disappeared.

Leo laid his brother's body on the ground; looking at him, still sobbing. Raphael kneeled by his brother's head, eyes closed, praying. Mikey adjusted the body, straightening the legs and folding the arms.

They mourned for their brother. This would be the last time they were all together.

Supernatural Exhibit

Supernatural is being above or beyond what is natural. It is unexplainable by natural law or phenomena. This is a broad definition. The pieces in this exhibit include haunted objects, haunted places, and demons. The supernatural qualities may be abundant or subtle. These pieces don't appear in other exhibits because of their unexplainable situations. One may consider creatures to be of the supernatural or may consider demons as a sort of creature. There is some overlap, but each piece rests in its most appropriate category. The Morbid Museum only employs experts in their fields of study.

The thought of life after death is a supernatural notion. Most of these pieces deal with a situation involving where one goes upon their demise. Will they haunt a place or person? Will they go to the fiery place or the peaceful one? Rest easy as visitors need not worry of their final resting place in our halls. These works may bring about questions of where one's actions may lead them. Listen and learn any lessons offered. There is no guidance when the end presents itself. These pieces attempt to remind everyone to enjoy the natural while they still can.

There is fun and excitement in observing the supernatural. Think of it as a controlled way of facing one's fears. Fear is healthy and all should welcome it. Fear is what keeps many alive. But fear can also result in a death. This is the final exhibit in our small museum. We do hope to expand. We thank our patrons. Many have been with us since we first began curating each exhibit. Visitors will embrace the unimaginable as they enter the Supernatural Exhibit.

Highway 491

I drove down Highway 491 in early June of 2008. My watch said 3 a.m. and I hadn't seen any other cars for at least an hour. I started to get that uncomfortable feeling. The one you get when things don't feel right; like something bad will happen. I looked out the windows up at the sky. I expected to see a bunch of bright lights flying around. I never believed in aliens, but for some reason I kept looking up.

I finally stopped looking feeling foolish. I put my eyes back on the road and I saw it. It felt strange that I didn't see it before; a circus tent with cars parked all around. Some of the cars looked old, but shinier than mine; like restored classics. I couldn't understand why a circus performed in the middle of the night.

Is my watch broken?

I had driven for a while and needed the rest, so I pulled over. I at least wanted to see the old cars from all decades; as much as 80-years-old.

I never saw a circus themed car show. After looking at a few of the classics, I went inside to see the show.

The smell of popcorn attacked my nose as I entered. I could feel something crunching under my feet though I didn't hear it from the loud music. Peanut shells covered the ground. An elephant in the center ring balanced things on its tusks. No one stood at the entrance, so I found myself a seat.

Everyone in the audience wore clothing from different decades. I didn't notice at first how strange people looked. When I saw a man with one of those curly mustaches throwing popcorn, I started looking at everyone. One section had a group of soldiers dressed in World War II uniforms. A bunch of flower power hippies threw flowers instead of

159

popcorn in another section. No one noticed me or any other people around them. The performances in the three rings hypnotized the audience.

I leaned over and spoke to the man next to me.

"What kind of show is this?" I said.

The man looked at me confused and uncomfortable. Without answering he returned to watching the well-trained elephant. After the elephant, a group of clowns ran out from behind the trainer and started goofing around. I decided I had stayed long enough and began to leave.

A man in a candy-striped jacket and straw hat stood at the entrance with an over exaggerated smile. He put one of his hands up.

"You cannot leave." He said.

"I'm sorry I didn't pay, but no one was around."

"Admittance is free, but you cannot leave."

The wide smile on his thin face and shrill voice made me uncomfortable.

"Why can't I leave?"

He snickered.

"It is almost time for the finale. You do not want to miss that."

He gestured for me to sit back down.

I returned to my seat but looked back every now and then to find the creepy man still standing there watching me. Before the clown act ended, I noticed a young man and woman walking into the tent greeted by the creepy man. I found it strange that the girl wore a blue shirt that said Clinton 2016. I took my chance and snuck out behind the creepy man while he spoke to the couple.

As I left, I could hear the Ringmaster on the loud speaker.

"Welcome you wondrous fools to the Sinister Circus!"

160

His deep voice continued to echo even after I escaped the tent.

"Now that our tent is full, we can continue with the show where we take your lives."

I got to my car. The crowd fell silent and the creepy man ran out of the tent. He saw me and started running. I hit the road as the horrific screams bellowed from the tent.

As I looked in my rearview mirror, the creepy man watched me next to the road as the tent vanished. A few seconds later the creepy man vanished. Part of me wanted to go back.

Was it real? Was it a mirage? A dream? I didn't want to know.

The sun started to rise. I looked at the signs by the road.

"Welcome to Utah!"

"New 491 Old 666."

Strange things happen on the Devil's Highway.

The Demon's Favor

I first met Mr. Yao at a political rally, although this meeting didn't occur in the conventional sense. Everyone attended the rally to raise money for street repairs. It didn't seem like the sort of thing anyone would protest against. But you never know what motivates other people.

Everyone's cheers and chanting fell. Muffled screams and load pops moved closer to the door. A man with a white beard crashed through the glass doors onto the floor.

"Everyone run! He's got a gun!"

Screams filled the room. Only the loud pops from the rifle broke through the screeching and yelling. I hid around a corner with two others. People fell like sacks of potatoes. Blood crawled along the grout between the tiles. Constant screaming. More rifle pops.

The active shooter turned towards me. I closed my eyes with my hands in the air; waiting. The screaming stopped; no noise.

Am I dead?

I waited a moment. Silence. I opened my eyes. Everyone stood frozen in place; like wax figures.

Is this death? Does time stop when you die?

That's when I met Mr. Yao. He walked up to me while everything else remained motionless.

"Good evening, Mr. Pion. My name is Mr. Yao. I have a proposition for you."

"What?"

"You see, you are about to get shot. I can stop this from happening. I can save your life."

"How? What's happening?"

"As you may or may not have noticed, I have stopped time. I can only hold it for a couple more minutes, so you must make a decision. Would you like to live…"

He pointed at the active shooter.

"...or die?"

"Of course, I want to live!"

"Excellent!"

With a smoky poof, a stack of papers and a pen appeared in Mr. Yao's hands.

"I need your signature before we can move forward."

I stared at the contract.

"What's the catch?"

"Simply this, I do a favor for you today and in return sometime in the future, I will call upon you to do a favor for me."

"That's it?"

"That is it. Nothing more and nothing less."

"What if I don't do your favor?"

"Then you die like you should have to today."

He remained calm and cool during the whole conversation. Everything about him looked pleasant except his smile; that wolfish grin.

Is this a lie so he can eat me?

"Time will be starting up soon, Mr. Pion. Sign or do not. It is your choice."

I walked forward, took the pen, and signed my name.

"Excellent!"

He turned the page.

"And sign here."

He turned another page.

"Initial here. Initial again. Sign here. Mother's maiden name. Sign again..."

"Can't I do this all with one signature?"

"And finally, stab your index finger with the pen and smear the blood on this page."

"What?"

"I am kidding. That is a terrible joke."

163

"What the hell, dude!?"

"Hey, lighten up Mr. Pion. I saved your life. And please do not call me dude."

With a puff of smoke, he was gone.

"NO!" The shooter said.

The rifle jammed. Police fired their pistols. The shooter dropped to his knees and the rifle fell to his side. He choked on his own blood and fell to the floor.

"The target is down! Move in!"

The shooter looked up at me, struggling for words.

"Your turn." He said.

***

Seven years passed, and I never thought of that day; a bad dream long forgotten. I lived alone, with my dog Max. I got home one evening excited to see my floppy eared friend.

"Hey Max. I got you a new bone."

"Hello Mr. Pion."

"Jesus Christ!"

With a lump in my throat and chest pounding, I grabbed the umbrella next to my door. Max put his head on the floor with his tail wagging in the air ready to play.

"Your jasmine green tea is delicious. And my name is not Jesus."

"Who are you? How'd you get in my house? How'd you get passed my dog? Why are you sitting in the dark drinking my tea?"

"I am very offended that you do not remember me, Mr. Pion. I only saved your life many years ago from a misguided shooter. But to answer your questions, you may recall my name is Mr. Yao. I come and go as I please, Max is unaware of my presence, and I'm waiting for you to turn the lights on. Allow me."

He snapped his fingers and the lamp next to him lit up. Max didn't acknowledge him and acted as if only I stood in the room.

"I apologize; I didn't recognize you."

"No harm; no fowl. Do you recall the agreement we made?"

With a poof, a stack of papers appeared in his hands.

"I owe you a favor, don't I?"

"Excellent memory, Mr. Pion. Yes, it is time to repay that debt. I am afraid you will not commit to what I am going to ask of you. Do keep in mind, by signing this document, you have already agreed to the undertaking. Would you like to review the contract before I continue?"

"I remember the agreement. Let's get this over with."

"Very well. Please sit down and enjoy this fabulous tea with me."

A cup of tea poofed onto the coffee table. I couldn't help but examine it before taking a sip. The aroma climbed up my nostrils with hot steam almost burning my nose. I burned my tongue and the roof of my mouth. It tasted sweet, as though Mr. Yao knew exactly how much honey I like in my tea. How did he make things appear out of thin air?

"Simply put Mr. Pion, in exchange for your life, you owe me another life. As I have said, you have already agreed to this and backing out now is not an option. We cannot go back in time to when you should have died so you must take a life. You can choose the life, or I can choose for you. I will give you one day to decide. I will return this time tomorrow."

Poof.

He vanished as quick as he appeared. The cup of tea left with him and Max never noticed things coming and going in my living room. The lump in my throat wouldn't go down and I felt nauseous. I'd never taken a life.

165

I couldn't sleep. Max snored all night on the floor. I felt anxious the next day. Small children even scared me.

"Hey, mister? Bang! Bang!"

"Steven don't point your toys at people!"

I walked by a movie poster covered with monsters and demons and a big, bold 'Coming Soon' on the bottom. Every time someone spoke, I heard something different.

"You gonna kill some people?"

"What!? What are you talking about?" I said.

"I said, do you have a light?"

"Oh! No, sorry."

I avoided everyone the rest of the way home. I didn't want to hurt anyone. I decided not to go through with the contract.

It must have a loophole.

I waited, wondering where Mr. Yao would appear.

"Hello Mr. Pion."

I never heard a poof. He stood by the front door.

"You have no idea what's happening, do you Max?"

"He is quite content with his half-devoured bone. Are you ready to proceed with our arrangement?"

"I...I don't thing I can do it. I've never taken a life before. I won't do it."

His wolfish grin disappeared.

"You have already agreed. You cannot break or alter the contract. In essence, all sales are final."

"But there must be something I can do. There must be some loophole."

"I am starting to lose my patience, Mr. Pion."

His clenched teeth should have warned me to agree, but I ignored this warning. Something I would soon regret. Mr. Yao's eyes turned red. The floor to my house disappeared and I fell through a tunnel made of skeletons and rotting corpses. I thought my skin burned from the heat,

166

though I had no marks. The stench of burning flesh overpowered my nostrils and I had to fight back the stomach acid in my throat.

I hit a hard surface causing an extraordinary amount of pain, but I could still move. Standing around me were beasts with waves of heat radiating off their bodies. It felt like I had ten blow dryers on high pointing at my face.

One demon with wings watched over everything from a cliff. He rested his arms on a large sword gleaming in front of his nude body. His face hid in the shadows, but I could see his horns protruding from his head. He spoke with a deep growl that shook the ground where I stood.

"You will follow the contract you signed in front of me. If you don't you will spend eternity getting torn apart by these creatures before you. Now go and await further instructions."

One of the monsters in front of me lifted an axe and swung towards me. That's when I woke up in my bed, sweating with Max at my feet. I would've brushed the whole thing off, but my living room wall had words burned into it.

AGREE OR BURN

Out of fear, I went to the only place I thought I could for help; a Catholic Church about a mile away. A priest should be able to help me more than anyone else, but would he believe me?

I ran in the church. The priest kneeled near the alter. The pews sat empty.

"Father? Father, I need your help!"

The elderly priest turned and looked at me with glazed, lifeless eyes.

"Agree or burn, Mr. Pion."

"What? No!"

I turned to see hundreds of people filling the pews, all chanting.

"Agree or burn! Agree or burn!"

My screams couldn't deafen the noise and I could still hear them as I raced down the street back home. I slammed my door shut and fell to the floor panting. I'd never run so fast. The room spun and made me dizzy. Any control of myself I had crept away.

Something seemed off as I laid on the floor. Something felt out of place. I realized Max hadn't come to the door like he always did when I came home.

"Max?"

Silence.

"Max! Come here boy, let's go for a walk."

Nothing. No panting or barking. No paws trotting through the kitchen. He loved walks, where could he be? To describe the nightmare on my bed would be uncomfortable. If I were to choose Hell over the contract, Mr. Yao demonstrated my eternal fate on my friend Max. So much blood.

I shut the door and sobbed on the hallway floor. I sat there for an eternity before Mr. Yao made another appearance.

"What will it be Mr. Pion?"

"You son of a bitch!"

I lunged for him. With a poof, chains wrapped around me and I hovered in the air. Every time I struggled; the chains tightened their grip.

"I have made it very clear what happens when I become cross with you so let us play nice. Agreed?"

I nodded.

The chains disappeared and my knees hit the floor first. I coughed too much to scream.

"I…agree…"

"As for the contract…"

"Yes…I…I will…do it…"

"Wonderful! But due to your recent insubordination, I will choose the lives you take."

And then he vanished. Why did he say lives? The nausea and pain caused me to black out. I don't know how long I slept.

My body ached when I woke. I found an envelope on my kitchen table. There were maps and charts, a business card for a rifle and ammo shop. There were print outs of tactical gear from online stores, and a letter from Mr. Yao.

Mr. Pion

Within the contents of this envelope you will find all the information you need to carry out your task. You must take the lives of everyone within the Premiere National Bank. I have included the Branch location, building plans, and demographic data.

You must get an assault rifle and tactical equipment to ensure your efficiency. You have three days to get your materials and execute your objectives. Upon completion of your mission, we will provide further details about your contract.

Sincerely,

T. Yao

T. Yao
Senior Manager
Living Contracts & Accounts Payable
666 W Styx Rd
Hades, Utah 66666-6666

Getting a rifle and the gear would be the hardest part with a three-day deadline. I thought some places had a waiting period before purchasing a firearm, but I had to try or else I'd end up like my poor dog Max.

I decided to stop by the bank first. There were four teller stations but only two were being used. An older, and fatter, security guard watched the bank floor.

Hidden behind his wrinkles were dark, sunken eyes. If his body failed, his eyes acted as sharp as ever. His trimmed mustache framed a pleasant smile he only showed to children. Everyone else he greeted with a polite hello but a cold, indifferent stare. He gave me the same look.

If I were to pull this thing off, he would have to go first. It felt unfair to take his life. But I guess fairness disappeared when I cheated death. I couldn't keep thinking about that. It would eat away at me, so I focused on the task. What kind of trouble would I have at the rifle shop?

"You here to pick up the rifle?" The clerk said.

"Yes, I'm here to buy a rifle."

"Mr. Pion?"

"Yes?"

"Okay. Please sign these forms. Only a formality. I'll be right back."

The clerk returned from the back room with an assault rifle I'd never seen before.

"You picked an excellent rifle Mr. Pion. This thing isn't even legal in California or Connecticut. It comes equipped with a night vision scope. Perfect for those early morning hunts before sunrise. Everything looks to be in order. Have a nice day sir."

"You don't need anything else from me?"

"No sir. You signed the forms, and we got a copy of your driver's license when you paid in full last week. You're all set."

"Okay, thank you."

"Thank you, Mr. Pion."

I couldn't remember being in that store. It had to be one of Mr. Yao's tricks. Did he control that guy like the men and women at the church?

When I got home, a package sat on my porch. It contained all the tactical equipment from the print outs. My name appeared on the box, but I never ordered it. Everything felt too convenient, like Mr. Yao had this all planned out before he ever came to see me. Before he killed Max.

I sat at my kitchen table staring at the building plans. I stared at the rifle, the ammo, the vest and ballistic plates, and Kevlar. Never in my life would I have considered any of this. The nausea rested in my stomach and never left.

I couldn't sleep that night. I still couldn't muster the strength to enter my room. The smell of blood and decaying meat escaped into the hallway. I couldn't even close my eyes without crying. Max always knew if I felt anxious and he would climb into my lap pawing at my face. I missed my best friend.

The morning came and went.

Then the afternoon.

Then evening.

I finally decided to stop thinking about it all and do it. I saw no way out. Some of the nausea subsided when I started making a plan. Enter here, do the business, exit here, drive away from here, ditch the car here. It reminded me of those spy movies. Everything felt easier when I didn't think about the people. You can't hurt people if you don't see them as people; only numbers, only obstacles in the way. No people here, no confliction of my humanity.

It's like playing Call of Duty.

They're not real, it's only a game.

No harm, no fowl.

171

Only a game.
The sun rose and I put all the gear on.
I'm a soldier going to kill bad guys.
Like Call of Duty.
Like a game.
I'm playing a game.
The crisp air visualized my breath in the chill of the morning. My breaths felt different that day; long, deep breaths every time. The transition from cold to warmth as I walked from the shade to the beaming sunlight felt extreme. I stood in the sun for a moment. I closed my eyes. I imagined myself wrapped in a blanket fresh from the dryer.

I saw no past.

I saw no future.

I saw only now.

With a deep breath, I loaded my car.

When I got to the bank, I sat there with the engine running. It was 9:23. I started thinking about the people inside.
Would the old security guard stop me?
How many people would scream or cry?
What would it say on the news?
Would I get caught?
Would they interview the victims' families?
Would I run out of bullets?
Would gun laws become stricter?
Would I live the rest of my life in happiness or regret and grief?
Would anyone come to my funeral?
Who will have to clean up my best friend's mangled body in my bedroom?

I started crying thinking of Max. I cried forever. I wiped my tears and cleared my throat. It was 9:25. I stopped thinking, grabbed the rifle, and walked to the door.

I saw the security guard through the window. I shot him before he saw me, shattering the glass door as he fell. The rifle deafened the screams and the breaking glass. My ear plugs deafened the gunfire. I heard nothing else. Everyone ran and fell and bleed out and died. I walked past ten bodies and saw a woman crouched down in a corner shaking. She shouted muffled words.

"Please don't kill me!"

As I squeezed the trigger, the rifle jammed, and she stood three feet closer to me.

NO!

I turned around to see three SWAT officers pointing their rifles. They shot, eighteen bullets all over my body and the ballistic plates. I saw the police escort the woman past me as I bled out on the floor. It's her turn now. I know she signed Mr. Yao's contact.

The last thing I see is Mr. Yao standing over me. I pull out one of my ear plugs.

"Ms. Pengo has taken your place. You should have read the fine print in the contract. You are still going to die, and you will burn. Enjoy your stay in Hell Mr. Pion."

He disappears. I inhale one final time as everything disappears.

Blue Ridge Mountain Hop

I don't care if any of you believe anything I say. You can call it one of those tall tales, but I know what I saw. It happened five years ago. I visited family back in East Tennessee. I hated listening to my drunk cousins complain about everything from politics to TV. I decided to try my luck at turkey hunting on the Blue Ridge Mountains. I took plenty of food and water to last the whole day, but I planned to go back home in a few hours.

I walked a lot and rested now and then hoping some poultry walked my way. I spent half the day with no luck hopping along the misty mountains. The sun started descending down the mountain and I decided to rest before humping back home. Plenty of sunlight remained but a chill crawled down the mountain. The chill rolled down my back dragging a shiver along the way, but it only lasted a second. Clouds blocked the sky and I thought a storm might hit me before I made it home.

I started my way home when I saw the first one. A man dressed as a Confederate Soldier dragging his rifle behind him. His dead stare looked at no specific thing. I thought he might be one of those reenactment boys.

"Hey buddy! You all right?"

He had no reaction. He walked past me, and I saw another Confederate far off. I turned to grab the first guy, but he vanished. I couldn't see him anywhere and no one stood behind any trees. He disappeared. Some pranksters are having fun with me, I thought.

Several soldiers wandered around now. One soldier walked towards me with his rifle pointing at me. He shouted but I didn't hear him. I couldn't hear anything. He thrust his bayonet at me, and I fell to the ground with my arm over my face. I'm ashamed to admit it but I screamed. Silence and stillness filled the air. I didn't feel anything, but fear prevented me from looking.

I finally opened my eyes and the soldier disappeared like the first one. I looked around and all the men had disappeared. I was alone again but I didn't feel alone. I could hear leaves rustling in the wind and squirrels rolled around in the grass. I ran home and never went back.

My cousins tried to take me out hunting last year and I said, "No thanks. I'm good right here." Go check it out for yourself if you want, but don't go hunting alone on the Blue Ridge Mountains.

National Paranormal Investigative Agency

The maid stumbled in panic. She made quick, short breaths running down the hallway. She looked back several times but saw nothing. She stopped at one door and pulled a card from her pocket. She put it in the slot on the door handle, but her hands shook too much. She dropped it. With a squeal, she picked it up and tried again. The small red light changed to green, and she opened the door. She slammed it shut, turned the lights off and squatted in a corner. She panted; tears running down her face.

She waited and listened. A gray transparent blob floated through the wall. She gasped catching the blob's attention. It laughed as lamps and books lifted in the air and flew after the woman. With a blood-curdling scream, she ran into the hallway. The gray blob followed. She stopped at the end of the hallway. She saw no escape. She turned and saw the blob moving towards her, still laughing. She fell to her knees and covered her face, whimpering. The blob crept towards her. A strange noise caused the blob to stop; a high-pitched ping sound that trailed off. The woman looked behind the blob towards the source of the sound.

At the end of the hall stood a man in a beige jump suit with large black boots and gloves. He wore a strange black backpack and goggles on his head. He held something with a cable attached to the backpack. The man distracted the blob. The woman ran into another room.

"You are so ugly!" The man said.

The blob bellowed a thunderous roar and charged towards the man. With a practiced comfort, the man pointed the device he held at the blob while repositioning his feet. He touched his ear and spoke.

"Third floor now! Third floor now!"

A female voice rang through the ear piece.

"Copy that! On my way."

He pulled the trigger on his device. An orange beam with a smaller red beam encircling it, lurched from the device and hit the blob. The beam wrapped itself around the blob. The blob tried to pull away. Instead of breaking free, the blob dragged the man. The man, leaning back, tried to pull the other way as his feet dragged against the carpet.

"This is new!"

The blob changed direction. The man fell backwards and the beam holding the blob disappeared. He heard it laugh disappearing through the walls.

A woman dressed in a similar beige jump suit trotted around the corner.

"Hal, are you okay?"

"Actually, I'm kind of comfortable."

"What happened?"

"A class five but seems stronger and smarter than usual."

"Stronger?"

"It dragged me down the hall when I hit it with the proton beam. It flew off that way."

"Description."

"Big, ugly gray blob laughs a lot. Smells like your last boyfriend."

She rolled her eyes leaving Hal on the floor. He rolled over and pushed himself up.

"Thanks for helping me up, Dina!"

Dina continued down the corridor ignoring Hal. He pulled down his goggles. Like night vision goggles, they zoomed in and out like photography lenses. He stopped for a moment and zoomed in on the wall.

"EP residue. Less than a minute old."

Hal zoomed in again. High-pitched laughter echoed from a distance followed by screams. A Chinese man in a business suit and no shoes ran around the corner almost falling over. He muttered something unintelligible to Hal and Dina pointing behind him.

Without a word, they trotted toward the screams and laughter. Their breath became visible and the temperature dropped.

"He's getting stronger." Dina said.

"I noticed."

Hal charged passed her. With a sigh, she followed.

Hal looked around through his goggles. He stopped in front of a door and pointed. Dina placed her hand on the doorknob. Hall primed his weapon. Dina nodded. Hal returned the nod. She pushed the door open and primed her weapon. Hal trotted through the door staying close to the wall. Dina followed turning down the adjacent wall.

The class five occupied itself with garbage. Dina rolled out a large box with a cord to the room's center. Hal hit the ghost with his beam. It screamed and pushed towards him. Hal let it push itself closer to the box on the floor. Dina shot her beam. It screamed again and tried to pull away. Dina stomped a button connected to the box. The box opened, and a bright light shot out around the class five. They both released their beams. The class five continued to struggle. The box sucked the blob inside, closed shut, and beeped three times.

Hal opened a Velcro pocket on his arm and removed a cell phone.

"Awesome! Right on time for lunch."

He reattached his weapon to the pack. Dina picked up the steaming trap. Hal stopped in the lobby and spoke with the hotel manager.

"I need your signature here on the invoice. This card has the contact information for the city's insurance policy to cover any damages. Questions?"

"I... I don't think so."

The hotel manager stood stupefied.

"Okay, well please call us if any strange things happen. We offer an affordable inspection service. We'll inform you before charging for other services."

"Okay. Thank you very much."

"You're welcome and enjoy the rest of your day."

The manager looked more perplexed with Hal's cheerful attitude. Dina waited in the company truck, a modified ambulance. Hal removed his pack with a sigh of relief and hopped into the driver's seat.

"Andrew left a message. Plaza Management wants their monthly inspection." Dina said.

She filed away the new invoice in the truck console.

"He prefers the name Bianca."

"Ugh, if he were going through a sex change, I'd call him Bianca. Dressing in drag doesn't make him a girl."

"Dina, he has a feminine personality. If he wants to identify as a girl named Bianca, then you should call her Bianca."

"His legal name is Andrew!"

"Then think of it as a nickname. It's not that big a deal."

"It's weird."

"We hunt ghosts for a living, and you think drag queens are weird?"

"Fine, I'll call him Bianca."

"Her."

"OKAY! Let's get lunch, do this inspection, and go home. Why do they request so many, anyway? Corporate suggests two inspections a year. Is the manager paranoid?"

179

"Something like that. It's the receptionist requesting inspections. You'll understand when you meet her."

They approached the front desk and the receptionist held up one finger. She spoke with a heavy southern accent.

"She's in a meeting. Can I take a message? Well all right, you have a nice day."

She put down the phone and looked at Hal with dreamy eyes and a smile.

"Hey Doll." She said.

"Hi Daisy. How are you?" Hal said.

"I'm wonderful, Darlin."

Daisy's cheerful tone changed when she saw Dina.

"Who's she?" She said.

"Oh, this is my partner, Dina."

"You guys are like… together?"

"What? No, she's my coworker."

"Oh."

Daisy removed a file from her desk and reviewed it.

"Someone said they heard noises in the janitor closet. They thought it could be mice, but we already had an exterminator come out, so I thought you could check it out."

"We'll get right on it."

Hal walked off. Dina stood for a moment replying to a text. When she looked up, Daisy glared at her.

"Have a nice day." Daisy said.

She was curt and rude. Dina hurried to catch up to Hal.

"Is this your monthly booty call?" Dina said.

"It's not a booty call. She's a kid with a little crush."

"Did you see the daggers in her eyes when she looked at me? That girl's obsessed with you."

"Like when you obsessed over Ian?"

180

"That was different. We had known each other for a couple years before I got a crush on him. That girl doesn't even know you."

"Are you threatened by her interest?" Hal said.

"I hate you."

"The closet is over here."

Hal opened the closet, pulled down his goggles, and looked at each shelf and the walls with care. He lifted the goggles and scanned the room with the EMF meter.

"So, how's this girl get away with calling for so many service requests?"

"Her uncle's the owner so she does what she wants as long as she can justify the business expenses. He always pays the invoices."

"If not for this place, Phoenix would have taken over months ago." Dina said.

"If they want to downsize so bad, why do they keep sending us people to train?"

"It's not about downsizing; Cushing wants us out of the way. And they send us new recruits because corporate still thinks you're the best."

"Cushing is behind all this? I hate that guy."

"Do you feel threatened by a black man in a leadership position?"

"I'm not threatened by an idiot. We started the same day, and he's a shady backstabber who only cares about making money. Corporate won't promote him so he wants to merge all the Arizona branches giving him control of the whole state. He wouldn't know what to do with a ghost if it slapped him in the face."

"You sound bitter. Are you sure you're not jealous of him getting promoted over you?"

"I never told you this Dina, but they offered me the job before Cushing. I turned it down because I wanted to stay in the field. That's why corporate sends me the new recruits. Even if they close down the Tucson branch, they'll put me in the training school out in New York. That'd be better than working for Cushing, but I'd also be closer to my parents. I love them to death, but I don't want to be in the same city."

Hal put the EMF meter away and closed the closet door. He wrote out the work order and handed a copy to Daisy.

"Thanks Doll." She said.

Daisy gave Dina a dirty look before returning to her computer screen.

"We need to get more calls if we want to stick around. Cushing is using our numbers against us." Dina said.

They were silent on the drive back to their office. Despite being mid-day, they were not likely to get any more calls. For Hal this meant tinkering with his prototypes or maintenance on old equipment. Dina spent the rest of her time returning phone calls. Bianca retouched her makeup when they arrived.

"How do I look?" Bianca said.

"Fabulous."

"Thanks Hal. I'm thinking of changing my name. There are too many queens named Bianca."

"I'm still gonna call you Andrew." Dina said.

"Well, I'll call you split ends." Bianca said.

Dina ignored the comment and went to her office.

"Have we heard anything from the recruit that's coming tomorrow?" Hal said.

"No one's called." Bianca said.

"Did the electronic parts I ordered come in?"

"No packages yet."

"Did you do anything today?"

"I painted my nails. Now they match my lipstick."

Bianca held her hands up and made a pouty face.

"It sounds like you've got your life together. I'm gonna put our new friend away. I'll be upstairs the rest of the day if anyone needs me. You stop working so hard."

"Never!" Bianca said.

The NPIA Tucson office had not had such an eventful day in months. Most days the staff of three struggled to find anything to keep them busy. The largest amount of paranormal activity concentrated in Phoenix. The Tucson office held charge over the southern half of the state. They never received enough calls. The majority of calls were pranks from students at the university. Dina researched the city and surrounding areas to determine why activity had dropped. No other office of the NPIA had encountered a loss in work.

The next day, Cushing arrived with the new recruit.

"Hi there. Can I speak with Dina and Hal please?" Cushing said.

"Yes, I'll go get them. Would you mind waiting here please?"

"Sure."

Bianca hurried to Dina's office, popped her head through the door, and then ran upstairs.

The recruit whispered to Cushing.

"Was that a…"

"Yes, it was." Cushing said.

Dina stepped from her office with an annoyed expression.

"Did you crawl out of your hole to deliver a recruit to us?" She said.

"Dina! How's Ian? Or did he get a restraining order?" Cushing said.

"He's too busy being the regional manager. Didn't you apply for that job?"

The smile fell from Cushing's face. He glared at Dina. Hal trotted down the stairs breaking the awkward silence.

"Now with you both here I'll get to the point. This is coming from corporate. You have thirty days to improve your business or they're putting me in charge. You will not lose your jobs, but you might have to transfer."

"I'm sure you'll see to our transfers yourself." Hal said.

"It's only business, Hal. Don't make this personal."

"Then why did you come down in person? A phone call or email would have been enough." Dina said.

"Ian asked me to tell you both in person. He said you would take the news better."

"Well, thanks for hand delivering the person; you may go now." Hal said.

"Don't get comfortable, kid. You'll get transferred before you're done training." Cushing said.

"He's wound a little tight. You think I should go help him relax?" Bianca said.

"He's straight." Dina said.

"So is spaghetti until it gets hot."

Hal shook his head.

"Welcome to Tucson, kid. That's Dina. Bianca. I'm Hal."

"Hi. I'm... I'm Mitchell. Or Mitch... um... yeah."

"Come on. I'll start you on equipment maintenance. We don't have a large crew here and it's good to know, anyway." Hal said.

"I can show him a few things."

Bianca winked at Mitch.

"No, Bianca!" Hal said.

Mitch hurried behind Hal. Bianca sat at her desk in a huff.

"So… that's like a… a dude, right?" Mitch said.

"You've never seen a drag queen before, have you? Don't worry. She flirts a lot, but she's harmless."

"What was… I forgot his name, what was his deal?"

"Cushing. He didn't get promoted so now he wants to merge the whole state into his office in Phoenix." Hal said.

"Is that good or bad?"

"Good for everyone in Phoenix; bad for the three of us down here."

"What are you guys gonna do?"

"We hope the numbers pick up in 30 days. That's all we can do."

"What's wrong with the numbers?"

"Not enough calls; not enough ghosts. Let's test your knowledge. What accounts for most ectoplasm manifestations?"

"Um… like negative emotions and stuff, right?"

"You don't sound too confidant, Mitch. Is that your final answer?" Hal said.

"Yeah. Yes. I'm sure."

"It is right; more or less. It's a combination of the deceased's emotions and the emotions of the living. What's unusual is our office covers the entirety of southern Arizona. The entire area has had a loss in activity. That's unheard of and no one can figure out why."

"That sucks." Mitch said.

"Yeah it does."

Hal led Mitch to a downstairs room.

"This is the containment room where we keep all the creepy critters. It's the standard class three system every agency office has. Although I made improvements to the storage capacity. I've been tweaking specs on a new model but I'm still waiting on parts to build a prototype."

"Handy guy."

"When you add to the storage, always wait for the green light before removing your trap. Once that's done, you write all the meter readings on this chart. For the weekly maintenance checks, you review the chart and make sure none of the readings were too low or too high. If that happens it usually means a processor needs replaced or bad cables or something. If not checked often, it will cause a breach of containment. All the negative ectoplasm will release."

"So, this holds negative ectoplasm. Could someone else collect it all before it manifests or whatever?" Mitch said.

Hal thought for a moment.

"It's possible, but they'd need to find it before manifestation. Oh! I have an idea. Mitch you're a genius!"

Hal ran upstairs.

"I… I did it. I made a good first impression." Mitch said.

"MITCH!"

"Oh! Mov… Moving."

Hal led Mitch to the second floor to his workroom. Hal ran to a table in the far corner. He shoved parts and equipment off except for one device. Mitch surveyed the room. He looked at everything as Hal removed and replaced small parts on the little device. Electronic parts and boxes covered a small bed. Disassembled gear laid all over the floor and on many shelves. Hal continued working and soldering as Mitch focused on a desk that looked out of place. The desk held books placed on end between two owl-shaped bookends. Books on electronics and paranormal research. One book lay on the desk with a receipt as a bookmark. Mitch picked it up and studied the cover.

"Night Shift?" He said.

"All right, Mitch. Mitch? Come here." Hal said.

"What's up?"

"I've been working on a way to track manifested spirits from a long range; trying to find them before we get a call. Thanks to your idea, I'm altering this to locate the ectoplasm in the pre-manifesting state. I'm not sure how well this will work, or if it will work, but it should help us figure out why there's less activity."

"Cool. So... what do we do?"

"First, we hook this little device up to the satellite on the roof. Then we test the wireless USB in the laptop to see what readings we get. Grab that laptop and follow me."

Hal sprinted out of the room. Mitch looked over and saw three laptops. He stood there motionless, unsure what to do. Hal sprinted back into the room.

"The laptop with the stickers on it."

Mitch gave a sigh of relief and ran after Hal with the stickered laptop. Hal attached the new device to the satellite controls. Mitch stumbled through the roof access door coughing and wheezing.

"Okay, Mitch, let me see the... Mitch? Hurry, dude!" Hal said.

Mitch trotted over passing off the laptop. He held his side and groaned after each cough. Hal paid no attention to Mitch's discomfort, typing away.

"Mitch. Hold the laptop; sit here and rest. I'm gonna turn the dish and set the controls. Tell me what the screen says when I finish."

Hal made the adjustments on the satellite dish.
"Anything?"

"Nothing on the screen." Mitch said.

Hal muttered under his breath. He double checked wire connections and the control panel.

"Shit. It might help if I turn everything on. Anything now?"

"Noth... wait... I got a map." Mitch said.

Hal took the laptop and reviewed the screen. Wrinkles formed on Hal's forehead.

"Either the device isn't working or there isn't any negative energy in this whole city. Hard to believe." Hal said.

"What's that green spot on the left side of the screen?"

"That's the mountain county park… which shouldn't be green on this map."

Hal zoomed and slid the screen over to reveal a large green blob covering most of the map west of Tucson.

"Damn."

"What? What is it?" Mitch said.

"Something is concentrating all the negative energy into that location."

"What's there?"

"Old Tucson Studios."

"What's that?"

"You've never been?"

"I'm from Flagstaff. This is my first time in Tucson."

"Well, that's where we're going. But according to this map that place is swarming with ghosts. Why hasn't anyone called?"

"I don't know."

"That was rhetorical, Mitch."

"Oh. No one's there? Nobody knows yet?"

"It's possible. I need to talk to Dina. We may not have enough people for this job."

"So, what do we do?"

"We go there and check the place out; do a little recon and see what we're up against."

Hal took off down the stairs.

"Again, with the running? Screw that."

Mitch walked towards the stairs with the laptop.

"Dina!" Hal said.

He flew down the stairs and passed Bianca into Dina's office. Bianca followed.

"He's gonna tell her he's in love with her." She said.

"We figured it out." Hal said.

Bianca let out a sigh of disappointment.

"What?" Dina said.

"All the negative energy is being focused at Old Tucson. Show her, Mitch. Mitch? Mitch!"

Mitch squeezed passed Bianca through the door and gave Hal the laptop. He showed Dina the map.

"Damn." Dina said.

"Ha. That's what Hal said." Mitch said.

"I'll take the kid to recon, but I don't think we'll be enough for this." Hal said.

"I'll go with you." Dina said.

"I want to send back data from the EMF meter to you here. This is new, and we need to log all the information we can."

"You sure this is accurate?"

"Are you asking me that right now?"

"It sounds like a legit question." Mitch said.

"Thank you, Mitch." Dina said.

"You realize you asked the biggest arrogant prick we know if he thinks he's right." Bianca said.

Hal clenched his teeth and restrained himself.

"Fair point; well made. Check it out. Keep the Com channels open." Dina said.

Mitch and Bianca buried away from the door as Hal left the office. He gathered gear and threw overalls at Mitch.

"Suit up. We leave in five." Hal said.

Mitch endured a bombardment of questions from Hal during the long drive. Hal tested his knowledge. All things he should have learned at the four-week training orientation. He asked technical questions, asked about dates in history, and the history of the company. Mitch's answers always had an air of apprehension.

They zigzagged down the mountain on Gate's Pass. Mitch pressed his right foot into the floorboard on the passenger's seat. Hal switched on the EMF meter mounted on the company truck. They saw nothing as the meter rotated. Hal parked the truck near the main entrance in the empty parking lot. The EMF meter showed bleeps and blobs while scanning a fifty-foot radius around the truck.

"This makes no sense. The EMF is showing complete manifested apparitions, but I see nothing. It's like something is manipulating the sensor." Hal said.

"Can a ghost do that?" Mitch said.

"I've never heard of one doing that. Let's look around; full battle rattle."

"Full what?"

"It means get all your gear on."

"Oh."

Hal gave Mitch a portable EMF. He checked the entrance and surrounding walls. Mitch noticed irregularities on the fence. The readings were beyond the sensor's range.

"What does this mean?" Mitch said.

"That means we're dealing with something stronger than any other ghost we've ever dealt with. Get back in the truck."

They both reloaded their gear. Hal started the truck and backed up to the far end of the parking lot.

"Why did you back up?"

"Being cautious. We need backup."

Hal called Dina. He typed on the EMF screen while he waited for her to respond.

"Hal are you guys there?" Dina said.

"I sent you our readings. This thing is off the scale. We need more people down here."

"I tried to call Cushing, but he's ignoring me. We're on our own."

"Give Bianca a pack. We need as much help as we can get. Mitch and I will keep observing until you get here."

"Copy that. Andrew... Bianca won't like this. We'll be there in about forty-five minutes."

"Now we sit tight. Keep an eye on the screen; I'm gonna take a nap."

"Uh... okay... um..."

Mitch felt uncertain if Hal had fallen asleep, but he had not moved. Mitch checked the screen on the EMF meter. No change. He looked out the window and sighed. The sensor released a high pitch beeping.

"Incoming!" Hal said.

Hal collected himself for a moment then shut off the beeping. He looked at the red dot on the screen in horror.

"Look!" Mitch said.

Far off in front of the theme park entrance stood a small figure wearing a cowboy hat and vest.

"Wh... what do you think it is?" Mitch said.

"Whatever's been sucking up the negative energy. Look at the screen. All the readings we had before have merged into one phantasm."

"And that's bad?"

"That's terrible. It's strong enough to kill us."

Another car pulled into the parking lot taking the ghost's attention away from Mitch and Hal. The car halted then reversed and skidded to a stop next to them. Bianca rolled down the window.

"What the hell is that?" Dina said.

"It's off the scale. This is all new. It's been sucking up all the negative energy. Does that car still have my black duffle bag?" Hal said.

"Yeah, why?"

191

"I got some new toys in there; haven't tested them yet. We'll try em out today."

"It's moving towards us!" Mitch said.

"Throw me the bag!" Hal said.

Bianca tossed him the bag as he stepped out of the car. He removed a metal ball, pressed a button, and over handed it towards the ghost flying after them. An orange glow filled the parking lot then dissipated. The ghost vanished. The EMF meter showed nothing on the screen. Everyone looked at Hal.

"That's a proton ball; a small blast to scare them away for a short time." Hal said.

"Let's gear up before it comes back." Dina said.

"So, what am I supposed to be doing?" Bianca said.

"Crash course in apparition apprehension. You get to be one of us for the day." Hal said.

"I didn't sign up for this. I don't even know how to use this stuff. The new guy knows more than me."

"Remember push, point, pull." Mitch said.

"Push this button to charge it, point this end at the ghost, and pull the lever. Too easy." Hal said.

"I have to carry this thing too? It's so heavy."

"Embrace the suck or let the ghost kill you. It's your choice." Hal said.

Bianca mumbled. Dina helped her with the gear. They walked towards the entrance. Mitch saw no readings on the EMF. A scream startled everyone as a proton beam set a poor defenseless cactus on fire. Dina, Hal, and Mitch all turned around to see Bianca breathing heavy and panting.

"Sorry. That was me. Sorry. Sorry Cactus."

"Why don't you walk ahead of us?" Dina said.

"Why?"

"I don't want to end up like that cactus."

Bianca hung her head and shuffled forward.

"Hit the lock on the fence, Bianca." Hal said.

She stood still. She muttered to herself as she went through the steps. She pushed the button causing the high-pitched ping sound. She took a breath then pointed her weapon at the gate. She pulled the lever. The proton beam bounced all over the gate and even part of the fence. She had no control. Hal stopped her and powered down the weapon. The gate fell to the ground, destroyed, with the lock still intact.

"Not bad for your first try." Hal said.

"You serious?" Bianca said.

"Yeah, you're doing great."

"Are you lying? Is he lying?"

Dina shrugged her shoulders. They entered the gate. Old Tucson looked like a small town lost in time, trapped in the desert. Dina held the EMF.

"We've got activity. They're all over. We should see something." Dina said.

"That's how it starts. They'll all merge into the thing we saw earlier. It could manifest anywhere. Dina get between us and keep watching the EMF." Hal said.

They walked towards the center of the small town; Hal at the front with Dina right behind him. Mitch on the left checking every corner as they passed buildings. Bianca followed behind. Her hands shook as she held her weapon. An unnatural silence crept along the street; no gusts of wind and not a cloud in the sky. Despite the sunny, clear day, a chill fell over them. The temperature kept falling. Everyone saw their breath as they exhaled.

"What's the reading?" Hal said.

"No change." Dina said.

The meter beeped, and a pulse knocked everyone down, disorienting them. The EMF fell silent.

193

"It's stronger than I thought. Four proton beams won't be enough." Dina said.

"I have a plan. There's no guarantee it will work but the four of us should be able to catch this thing. The proton blast weakens them making them run away. If we can get a beam around it, the blast should weaken it enough for us to trap it." Hal said.

"And you think it'll sit there and let us blow it up!?" Bianca said.

"One beam will give it a tickle. It won't care. If we get the blast off while the beam's on it, it won't be able to disappear." Hal said.

"I don't like this plan." Mitch said.

"You got something better!?" Dina said.

Mitch and Bianca shared apprehensive glances as Hal and Dina got the trap ready. No one said anything while they waited for the ghost to return. The temperature dropped again.

"Everyone get ready." Hal said.

A low voice echoed through the theme park.

"You will die!"

"Everyone power on!" Dina said.

The high-pitched ping sounded like an echo as everyone switched on their proton packs. Objects levitated and circled them. The cyclone of items gained speed as more objects joined the frenzy. The ghost appeared behind Dina.

"Bianca hit him!" Dina said.

Bianca fired and missed. A chair flew out of the cyclone knocking Bianca down. This gave Dina time to roll over and fire a proton beam. The ghost disappeared. The cyclone gained speed. Objects left the collective and attacked each person.

"Mitch, 6 o'clock!" Hal said.

Mitch jumped around to see the ghost in front of him. He fired his proton beam and caught the ghost. It laughed. Mitch flew several feet and his proton beam broke loose. The ghost continued laughing. Dina looked at Hal. They both nodded. They both fired a proton beam. The ghost deflected Hal's beam giving Dina's beam the advantage. Hal threw a proton grenade. The cyclone stopped. The objects fell. Hal shot another beam catching the ghost. They both struggled.

"We can't hold it! Mitch get another grenade!" Hal said.

"Bianca shoot it!" Dina said.

Bianca shot a beam and hit the ghost. They struggled. Mitch stumbled over to Hal and rummaged through his bag. He found the last proton grenade and threw it. The three pulled the ghost towards the trap as it fought against them.

"Mitch hit him!" Dina said.

Mitch shot his proton beam. The ghost screamed. It kept fighting, but the four pulled it closer to the trap. When the ghost finally hovered over the trap, Dina hit the button. A flash of white light flew from the trap. The ghost kept fighting. The four covered their eyes. The trap pulled the ghost down.

The trap shook a few times as it beeped with a flashing red light then stopped. Everyone panted as they stared at the steaming trap.

"So, are we done? Can we leave now?" Bianca said.

"If the EMF shows no activity, then yes we can go." Dina said.

"I'll meet you guys at the car. I'm gonna sit for a minute." Mitch said.

"We gotta get you in shape, Mitch." Hal said.

The next day, Bianca sat behind the front desk claiming never to return to the field. The EMF showed normal activity, and they had already received one call for the day.

"I got an email from Corporate this morning. They want all the data we have from yesterday. They're also letting us keep the Tucson branch." Dina said.

"I bet Cushing's unhappy right now." Hal said.

"Corporate is opening an internal investigation. They think it's strange we didn't notice sooner. The entire state is under a fine-tooth comb."

"Sounds like my parents got my message. My dad is the CFO. He and my mom have been around since the beginning. That's why I never wanted to work at the corporate office. I wanted to follow my own path. I also didn't want to people calling me Mr. Tulley."

"Hal, is that why you turned down all those promotions? You think your dad pulled strings for you?" Dina said.

"I didn't want to find out." Hal said.

"Hal, Daisy called and said they have a real ghost this time. She's all panicky and sobbing. It sounds like the real deal." Bianca said.

"Load up the car, Mitch. Daisy might fall in love with you if you save the day." Hal said.

"What!?" Mitch said.

"Nothing."

The Dragon Sanction

People are running; screaming. Electricity ricochets through the clouds, the air, and any metal along the block. Houses and cars are burning. Power lines lay in the street. The number of people running matches the number of corpses on the ground. Chaos. Destruction. Moving towards the street's center. A black, charred, steaming mass lay in front of a small child. The child cries.

"I'm sorry, daddy. I didn't mean to."

Lighting shoots from the child's hand into the black mass. The child screams.

***

A man awoke with heavy breathing. The clock next to him read 5:57 a.m.

"I hate it when I wake up before the alarm."

He sighed and rubbed his face.

He staggered to the kitchen; yawning. He placed a kettle on the stove. A black cat brushed against his leg as he got a tea bag from the cabinet.

"Oh, hello. Forgive me for not feeding you first thing. Or you want water. That's almost empty. Did you drink a lot of water or did I forget to fill it? You're a riveting conversationalist, Bagheera."

He turned on the television listening to the broadcast as he filled the cat's bowl and the tea kettle.

"The League of Nations began their peace talks yesterday afternoon. Meeting representatives from the United Nations of the Americas and the United Orient. The UNA and the UO split from the League shortly after World War II. They claimed the League was too weak and failed to prevent the war. Rumors had circulated of creating a new stronger global governing body. The three main countries; the United

197

States, Great Britain, and China, each had their own ideas. They split into factions and the war of global politics began.

"70 years later, they are coming together to create that unified global organization. Top officials will continue negotiations outlining the details of the new plan. They will announce this new plan at the Global Peace Summit two weeks from today."

The man showered and dressed after his tea. He buttoned a navy-blue work shirt. The name on the shirt read Victor. He sighed looking in the mirror.

"Get through today. Worry about tomorrow when it gets here. Focus on today. Today is going to be a great day. Shit."

He removed two pills from a prescription bottle and swallowed them dry.

"I hate this job."

***

"Okay, Jessica, start at the beginning of the dream then tell me when you get to the new stuff."

"Well, it always starts the same. I'm standing in a neighborhood. I don't know where. I've never been there before. People are screaming and running. I see bodies lying everywhere. Power lines are sideways. Houses and cars are on fire. There's an electrical storm or something but I don't see a lot of clouds. It's not raining. Electrical sparks are all over. This is the new part. There's a little boy in the middle of the street. He can't be more than four or five. He's standing in front of something. A charred something. It's large. It might be a person; the boy's mother or father. The boy's crying. He says something but I can't hear. Then I wake up. What do you think it means, Amy?"

"For most people I would say we need to see the dream through before making assumptions. In your case, with your abilities, you might be dreaming the same thing as someone else. You said you've never had dreams like this."

"Not this vivid. I've had visions as dreams, but they were cloudy and disconnected. This feels more like a memory. And I'm usually in my dreams. I'm not in this one."

"You might be dreaming someone's traumatic past. They haven't dealt with the trauma and you're picking up on the heightened emotional energy."

"Who would I be connecting with? I've never heard of an incident like this. It feels too surreal to be more than a dream."

"Some memories manifest as dreams. They may include unrelated details or parts from other memories. This dream could be a combination of memories."

"I've only seen other's memories after I touch them. How am I seeing this when I'm asleep?"

"We call the segment of sleep when people dream Rapid Eye Movement or REM sleep. It mimics brainwaves like the waves when people are awake. The difference is all your other brain activity has shut down. Your empathetic abilities may heighten in this state. You might sense other's emotions at a distance. With this dream, it's coming from someone who's emotions are stronger and your mind is focusing on this."

"How do you know it's not a random dream?"

"This doesn't fit with anything we've discussed here. If it were only a dream, it's so unusual, I wouldn't know where to begin to unravel it. Aaron and Ama are my only other patients with abilities and there's do not compare with yours. I've spoken with colleagues about their patients with abilities in Europe and it's the same."

"I know the people you're talking about. We're a small group. What about our counterparts in the Orient?"

"They're not open to sharing information. I suspect, from videos I've seen, they don't come close to what you're capable of. We're only scratching the surface of what you can do. Stay focused. Remember, structure will keep you safe."

"I remember. This dream is out of routine and I don't understand it. It's making me flustered."

"I understand. How's everything else?"

"Not bad. Not great. Work is fine, nothing stressful. Nothing exciting is going on in my personal life which is for the best right now. I haven't been with anyone in almost a year."

"That's a longtime for you."

"It feels like a lifetime. I don't even feel like the same person I was a year ago."

"How do you feel about that?"

"It's great. I love the person I've become, but it feels lost. It's like, okay, I'm this new person but what does she like to do? I have to discover myself all over again. It's like when I first accepted that I had these abilities. I had to learn how to live again. It's like I was reborn."

"Like a phoenix from the ashes."

"Exactly. You should know, you're the first doctor I've had I actually liked. And I've had a lot of doctors."

"Well I'm not here because the government pays me. You're a wonderful person and I want to see you reach your full potential. You're going to change the world and I'm not saying that because you have special abilities. You can change the world with or without them."

"You're going to make me cry. Thank you. For saying that. It feels like a good day."

"I'm glad I helped make your day better. Now, keep to your schedule. It's time for lunch."

***

"How is everything?" The server said.

"Delicious. Everything's great." Victor said.

"Let me know if you need anything."

Victor ate a chicken salad with avocado, apple slices, and raspberry vinaigrette. Jessica entered the restaurant looking at her phone distracted. She bumped into Victor's table, spilling his water and dropping her phone and bag.

"Oh my God! I am so sorry. I wasn't paying attention."

"It's okay. I hope your phone isn't broken. Let me help you."

"You don't have to do that. It's my own fault. Can I pay for your lunch?"

"Not necessary. It was an accident. I've had many accidents."

"You're very nice. I have lunch here every day, but I don't think I've seen you before."

"First time here. Trying something new."

They both grabbed a piece of paper; their fingers toughing. Victor's memories flashed within Jessica's mind like clips in a movie reel.

Victor, a teenager, lays in a bathtub. His wrists cut and bleeding. His body becomes limp; motionless. Electrical sparks fire from his wrists and through the water. He gasps for air. Breathing heavy, he looks at his arms. The wounds have cauterized. He screams at his arms.

Victor, 10 or 12-years-old, pets a stray cat. The cat is affectionate. Victor looks happy. Electrical sparks fire from Victor's hands. The cat dies. Victor cries and apologizes. He holds the cat carcass rocking back and forth.

Victor, 4 or 5, stands in a street. He's the child from the dream. He apologizes to the charred mass. He caused the electrical storm. He killed his father.

201

Jessica caught her breath. She shook.

"Is everything okay?" Victor said.

She pulled the sleeve up on Victor's arm revealing the scar on his wrist. He pulled his arm away and stood. He left throwing money on the table.

"Wait! I'm sorry. Please let me explain."

Jessica scrambled to collect her things. She ran outside. Victor had gone. She closed her eyes. She turned with confidence and made a call.

"Aaron. It's Jessica. I've found another one. I'm pursuing him now. Another one of us. Someone with abilities. Electricity, I'm guessing. I know I'm not a field agent. I bumped into him getting lunch. I'm certain he's not with the UO or the League. One hundred percent. I'll explain everything. Get Ama and come find me. Okay. See you soon."

Jessica turned a corner and saw Victor several blocks away. She dialed another number.

"Colonel. This is Ether. Earth and Water are coming to me. The Dragon Sanction is active. I repeat. The Dragon Sanction is active."

She followed Victor further. The area became more populated. She lost him in the crowd. She closed her eyes. She sensed him; his powers. She sensed others. Danger.

The Sapphire Cat

1

Where am I? I'm on a road. That's a car with the trunk open. Whose car is that?

The man struggles to stand, picking himself up from the asphalt. He gets to his feet and doubles over, retching on the car and the street.

What's my name? Amnesia. Vomiting. Head throbbing. Concussion. I have a concussion. Who am I? Wallet. Driver's License. John Adler. My name is John Adler. 1634 Racine. I have business cards? Detective John Adler. Private Investigator. I'm a detective. Why am I here? Is this my car?

Adler searches his other pockets and puts the contents on the hood of the car. There is a note with an address, 388 Fenton Street, and a shipping invoice. Adler's wallet has twenty-three dollars and four business cards, a receipt from Sheri's Diner. But no car keys. Adler tries the door handle; the car is open but no keys in the ignition. He looks in the glove compartment to find insurance and the registration in his name for the vehicle. He finds a light bulb for a vehicle tail light and the receipt for the light bulb. He also finds a receipt for an oil change and a bottle of acetaminophen. He takes two of the pills from the bottle. He checks the floor board but finds nothing.

Where are my keys?

He stands from the car and gets overcome by severe dizziness. He holds the car for balance and his stomach to fight the nausea. Adler is unsure how long he stood waiting for the dizzy spell to pass. He collects himself and walks to the back of the car. No keys in the trunk lid keyhole.

Did the keys fall in the trunk? Why was the trunk open? The tire iron. Did I change a tire? No. There's no spare. I helped someone else change a tire.

A faint memory returns to Adler as he stares at his trunk. He stands there trance-like as the images come to him. A short, portly man, waving his arms next to a car with hazard lights flashing.

"I don't have a jack and I got a flat tire. Do you have one I can use?" The portly man asked.

Adler sees himself under the car working the jack. He hears the man from far off.

"I appreciate your help. I think three cars drove right passed me before you."

Adler sees himself shaking hands with the portly man.

"What was your name again?"

Adler sees himself driving away from the man.

I drove away. I had another reason to open the trunk. Where are my keys?

Adler surveys where he woke. He lays down and looks under the car. There his keys lay, and he claims them. He stands too fast and feels another dizzy spell. He holds the trunk lid for support. Several minutes pass.

I can't drive like this. How can I go home if I don't know where I am? I can't risk a car accident while I have a concussion. I can leave the car here for the night. I better make sure there's nothing important inside. It doesn't look like anything important is in the trunk. There's only a newspaper in the back seat. It doesn't look old. Maybe that's today's paper. Museum break in?

Another memory fades into his mind. He knows it is that day's paper, and he knows about the break in. This memory is not like the one before. This memory is clearer. Adler was paying attention when this all happened. He received a call from a colleague asking for help. The police were investigating the break in, but nothing was missing.

***

The phone call was brief. Adler never liked talking on the phone.

"Adler, it's Dean. I need a favor."

"I'm listening." Adler croaked through the receiver.

"We got a break in at the museum warehouse but nothing's missing. I need someone with sharper eyes than mine. How soon can you get here?"

"Give me twenty minutes."

Adler looked at the cat sitting on the coffee table staring at him.

"Wanna go outside?"

The cat leaped towards the sliding glass door with a trill.

"You better get done before I leave."

He dressed for the day in the usual garments; black shoes, black slacks, gray button-down shirt, no tie. He never wore ties. He did not bother with shaving. He liked how his face looked with a short, trimmed beard but was too lazy to clean the stubble on his neck. He slid a suit jacket over his arms and broad shoulders. He stood in front of a mirror and adjusted the sleeves under the jacket. His wide chest and thin waist gave a triangular appearance to his tall body.

He sipped a cup of coffee as he waited for the cat to return inside. This was the normal morning ritual. The only difference from any other day was the phone call from Detective Sergeant Dean. It was not uncommon for Dean to consult with Adler, but it was rare for someone to ask him to view a crime scene in person.

Detective Dean was waiting for Adler when he arrived. He was taller and thinner than Adler with a shaved face, brown suit, light blue shirt, and a dark red plaid tie.

Officers would say they were opposites. Adler had known Dean since high school. They were not close, but he was the closest thing Adler had to a friend. They choose different career paths but found themselves in the same profession.

Dean always wanted to be a police officer. He applied for the academy on his twenty-first birthday. He never planned to be a detective, but the opportunity came, and he took it. He was a good detective and closed more cases than most.

Adler went to college. He had always been the intellectual one and wanted nothing more than to leave home. His foster father was an abusive drunk. His foster mother had a mental disorder she refused to take medication to subdue. This prompted Adler to study psychology and Criminal Psychology. After college, he spent three years working for a private investigator. He started his own agency shortly after. He proved to be more capable than other detectives. Most of his income came from police consultation.

Neither man said a word as they entered the museum. Most of the officers had met Adler, but no one spoke or approached him. He preferred being alone. Dean did not bother him with small talk because he knew Adler would have no interest. He focused instead on the facts of the case.

"Someone disconnected the security cameras just before three in the morning. The janitor and security guard were on the other side of the building. We're still looking into whether they were accomplices. This way." Dean said as he guided Adler down a service hallway to the warehouse and loading dock.

They entered a large room with concrete floors and no windows. The roll-up door from the loading dock was up providing light from outside. Adler did not notice or care if they illuminated the light fixtures. There were boxes and wooden crates scattered and stacked in random patterns.

206

Many of the crates sat busted or cracked open but none of the contents appeared to be missing. Packing peanuts, bubble wrap, straw, and sawdust spilled out of the crates. Adler made no attempt to hide the agitation on his face.

"Someone's already compromised the scene. Museum workers checking the inventory, I assume." Adler said.

"Yes, before reporting the break-in. The call came at 5:34 a.m. The guard says he noticed the break-in at about five in the morning. They said nothing was missing."

"Someone was looking for something. I'm guessing they didn't find it." Adler said.

"We're thinking drug smuggling. I'm waiting for the museum director to get the shipping information so we can figure out where they came from."

"It's not drugs. All the crates they opened are from Madagascar. It's printed on the side. I suspect jewels or precious gems. We need to talk to whoever accepted the shipment. They probably didn't add something to the inventory."

"That's why I'm waiting on the museum director. He said the warehouse manager hasn't been to work for a couple days. He didn't think it related to the break-in because the guy talked about quitting. They said he hated the job. I was planning to run by the guy's house when I finished. You can tag along."

"Any shipments come in the last day he was here?" Adler asked.

"There may have been. The director is in the office. Let's go ask."

The director was going through folders and throwing papers every which way.

"How could anyone find uh, uh damn thing in this disorganized mess?" The director said.

He was a short, thin man in a gray three-piece suit. He had snow white hair with a neat, trimmed mustache. He did not move in a hurry but made up for this with a hurried stammer when he spoke.

"Th-this used to be uh, uh well organized museum of uh, uh stature. Then they hired uh, uh bunch of damned, damned hippies. Oh, oh detective, I'm sorry. I'm, I'm still looking. There's nothing filed in this whole place. It'll take weeks to, to sort this out." The director said.

"Doctor Stanton, this is my associate, Detective Adler. Were there any shipments delivered on the last day your warehouse manager worked?" Detective Dean asked.

"I, I don't know. That's what we paid the damn uh, uh manager for."

Adler looked over the office desk as he spoke to Doctor Stanton.

"Do you know what they delivered from Madagascar?"

"Statues and uh, uh pottery mostly. That's what we purchased so we can expand the African exhibit."

Doctor Stanton continued throwing papers and muttering to himself.

Adler picked up a note with an address, 388 Fenton Street. He pocketed the note and looked at a stack of shipping invoices. The third paper listed fifteen crates from Madagascar.

"How many crates did they break open?" Adler asked.

"Fourteen and museum staff confirmed no crates were missing." Dean said.

"The invoice says there were fifteen crates dated two days ago. See if they misplaced the crate or left it off the inventory."

"Th-this rat's nest of an office. I don't even know what uh, uh this is."

"Doctor Stanton, we found the invoice. Could you make a copy, please?" Adler asked.

"Oh. I... sure. I'll uh, uh send someone in to clean this place up."

He walked away then shuffled back.

"Was that on the uh, uh desk the whole time?" Doctor Stanton asked.

"Yes, sir." Adler said.

"Oh."

Doctor Stanton held his confused expression. He passed Detective Dean out of the office.

"I'll bring the security guard in to help us check the inventory." Dean said.

Adler checked the note in his pocket. He knew Fenton Street had several warehouses and empty buildings.

"The guard says they only checked in fourteen crates from the last shipment." Dean shouted around the door.

"Let's find that employee. I'll follow a lead and let you know what I find." Adler said.

"What are you thinking?"

"The missing manager was trying to fence something valuable. Or he planned to and the original buyer broke in to find it. Call me when you find the guy."

***

That explains the invoice and the address. When did I get the newspaper? I guess I should lock up the car and walk.

Adler locks his car and looks down both ends of the street. He is debating which direction to walk. There is nothing in either direction. He walks the opposite way his car is facing. There is nothing illuminating the street except moonlight. He has no sense of time. He could walk for hours or minutes. He guessed he had walked for thirty to forty-five

209

minutes. He stops at the top of a hill or mountain; he is not sure which. He sees the city below. He also sees the hospital. It is close.

They can check me out and make sure I'm okay. Maybe I can piece some of this day back together. How does the guy with the flat tire relate to anything? I need to get my thoughts together before I get to the ER. Do I even have insurance? I guess it doesn't matter.

He starts his downhill walk along the road to the hospital. He predicts it will take less than an hour. His body reminds him of hunger and thirst. No memories are coming back. He is focused on survival. There is a chill in the air, but the weather is not uncomfortable. From far off, he sees a few cars roaming the streets. He assumes it is early morning. It reminds him of his favorite time at night, before everyone wakes up; before twilight. And after all the criminals venture home to sleep during the day. Adler's favorite time lasts about an hour when the city is at peace and there is no one around. He thinks of it like a graveyard; silent and serene.

Almost there. I'll get help then I can focus on remembering how I got here. Why was I in the middle of nowhere? Why did I open the trunk? What caused me to pass out? I hope it's not a tumor.

2

Adler parked in front of the roll-up door at 388 Fenton Street. The door next to the roll up was not locked. Ever vigilant, he opened the door enough to listen inside. Silence. He crept in, pausing to let his eyes adjust.

I should've got lunch first.

Two black SUVs faced two more with bodies between them. He moved forward slow and quiet. With every breath, the smell grew stronger.

These guys have been here for a while.

Adler removed his handkerchief from his inside jacket pocket and covered his nose. He inspected one body. The body wore a blood drenched expensive suit, a gold necklace, and rings. The body held a pistol in its right hand.

He unloaded the whole clip before going down. It looks like they all did. But someone left a suitcase.

Adler approached the suitcase and the body nearest it. He tried to open it with his handkerchief. It opened, containing stacks of cash. Blood got on his handkerchief.

Dammit. Glad I've got more at home. So, if there's cash here, what were they buying?

He surveyed the rest of the scene. One side had two SUVs, the cash, and eight dead men. The other side had two SUVs, seven dead men, and a trail of blood drops leading between the SUVs. A small pool of blood sat behind one of the SUVs with another trail leading to a back door.

I bet the museum clerk is the one who got away. Dean will want to see this.

Detective Dean arrived twenty minutes later with a couple uniform officers.

"Jesus! It's a damn bloodbath. What the hell is this?"

"I'm betting these guys were here to buy whatever is in that missing crate. Something went wrong, maybe someone got paranoid. There's a trail of blood that goes outside. One guy got away, probably with the crate." Adler said.

"It looks like the mob. This case is getting complicated. I'm glad I pulled you in."

"Why did you pull me in?"

"To be honest, you've always enjoyed this stuff. That's why you're good at it. I don't care anymore. I want to move to a desk job. That'll make Jeanie happy too. She's always worried I'll get shot and my mother-in-law gets her riled up and she'll call me every half-hour to check on me."

"So, you want me to do the work for you?"

"Yeah, pretty much."

"Okay. Let's get forensics to ID that blood and get fingerprints. I want to know if our missing guy is our museum guy. I'm gonna see if I can figure out which gangs these guys are from. This could be a turf war."

"I may not like it, but I know how to do my job, John. I've got things covered here. You better get some lunch. This one's gonna take a while."

"You lose faith in me already?"

"Even you aren't that good."

After lunch, Adler drove to the Vero Italiano Restaurant.

"Good afternoon, Sir. Will you be dining alone?" The concierge said.

"John Adler. I'm here to see Carlo."

The concierge took the business card to the back of the restaurant, then returned a few minutes later.

"Mister Valentino will see you."

Adler walked to the table closest to the kitchen. One man sat alone at the table with a plate of pasta and a glass of red wine. Behind him stood two men, in expensive suits, the size of gorillas. One with a beard and one without. The man at the table wiped his mouth with a napkin and stood. He wore a gray three-piece suit with the jacket on the chair next to him.

"John."

"How are you, Carlo? How's your mother?"

"For an 85-year-old woman, she's still meaner than Hell. Please sit down. I hope you don't mind if I eat my lunch. What can I do for you my friend?"

"Do you know anything about a warehouse at 388 Fenton Street?"

"It's not one of mine. We only got the 500 block through 800 block on Fenton Street; fishing and textiles that sort of thing."

"Do you know who owns it?"

"Unless he sold it, it should belong to Bulger, that fancy finance guy downtown. I don't know nothing about what they do there."

"We found some guys in your business there this morning. All dead, a couple days old."

"We missing any guys, Jimmy?"

"No, Sir, Mister Valentino." The bearded gorilla said.

"Not our guys. You should ask Bulger."

"You do any work with them?"

"Nah. Rumor is they're into drugs and human trafficking. I keep my distance. Those are rumors though."

"They ever fence jewels or art?"

"Bulger's crew? Ha! Jimmy here knows more about art than they do. What do jewels and art got to do with this?"

"That."

Adler pointed to the newspaper on the table. The museum break in covered the front page.

"That?" Carlo said.

"Something tells me they're connected."

"Gallow. He's Bulger's biggest rival. Don't know if he's into art, but they may have a reason to have a beef with Bulger."

"Thanks. I owe you."

"Nah. Don't worry about it. You helped my brother-in-law get out of a tight spot. You're almost family."

"Until I piss you off."

"You gotta do somethin really stupid to piss me off. And you ain't stupid. Come by anytime."

213

"Mind if I keep this paper?"

"Go ahead. I'm done with it."

Adler noticed a woman at the bar as he left. She was blond, thin, wearing a maroon dress with matching lipstick and nail polish. She glanced at him with a look that asked him to buy her a drink. He gave no expression showing a strong no.

Sorry, honey. I've got too much to do today.

He drove across the city towards downtown. Bulger had several successful operations and owned several properties in the finance district.

"I need to speak with Jesse Bulger." Adler said.

"Mister Bulger is in a meeting. May I take a message?" The receptionist said.

"Call upstairs and tell them Detective John Adler is here. It's about a property Mister Bulger owns."

"I'll see if someone can come down. Have a seat if you'd like and help yourself to some water."

"Thank you."

Adler explored the lobby. A security guard stood by the elevator and stairs. Near the receptionist's desk sat a brown leather couch and glass coffee table. Outdated golf and finance magazines covered the table. Next to the couch sat a small refrigerator filled with bottles of water. He overheard the receptionist whisper into her telephone.

"There's a detective here to see Mister Bulger. He says it's about a property the company owns. He didn't say. Okay. Yes."

Adler pretended to look at the magazines as the receptionist approached him.

"I'm sorry Mister Bulger is still unavailable. Mister Willis is coming down and he can help you with anything you need."

"Thank you."

I love when people think I don't understand their screening process.

Adler waited for twenty minutes. He saw the security guard yawn, and the receptionist read a gardening magazine. The security guard took water from the mini-fridge and returned to his post. The elevator opened. The security guard nodded to the man who exited.

"Detective. How may I help you?"

"Mister Willis? John Adler."

"Yes. A pleasure. I understand there's a problem with one of our buildings?"

"Does your employer own a warehouse at 388 Fenton Street?"

"He might. We have a couple warehouses on Fenton Street, but I can't be sure of which ones off the top of my head."

"I'll need you to confirm that. Police found bodies at the warehouse this morning."

"I see. Meghan, can you call finance and ask if 388 Fenton Street is one of our assets?"

"Yes, Sir." The receptionist said.

"We will assist any way we can, Detective."

"Thank you. I like the paintings you have in the lobby."

"Ah, yes. Mister Bulger has quite the eye for fine art. He recently financed the acquisition of several statues and figures from Madagascar. He donated them to the city's museum."

"I appreciate it when the wealthy give something back to the community."

"Indeed. Mister Bulger donates to many non-profits. Those donations created two thousand jobs last year."

"Mister Willis? They said it is one of our properties."

"Thank you, Meghan. Well, I'll do my best to answer your questions, Detective."

"Have you had any reports of missing staff or break ins?"

"None. I'm the VP of operations. Those reports would have come across my desk."

"Well, it's possible these people broke in to the warehouse. I'll come back if I have more questions."

"I hope you catch whoever killed those people."

"Why do you assume I'm searching for a killer?"

"I thought you were here because you found corpses."

"I never said anything about murder."

"Do you even know the cause of death?"

"I'll be in touch Mister Willis."

Adler called Detective Dean.

"Dean. You get an ID on any of the bodies?"

"They're not local. Haven't found any ties to our city yet. The blood is at the lab getting tested. You got anything yet?"

"A little. Not enough to justify a warrant. You know anything about Jesse Bulger?"

"The finance guy? If I had anything on him, I'm sure he'd buy his way out. I'll see what we got. Hey, Johnny hold on a sec."

Adler listened to the muffled words. Nothing was clear.

"Johnny, we got a body. Gunshot wound in the arm but not the cause of death. It might be our missing museum guy. Head over to the tow yard west of highway 70."

"Got it. I'll be there in about 20 minutes."

Adler turned down the dirt road with a cloud of dust trailing behind. He parked among the patrol cars. Detective Dean waited for him by the gate.

"Positive ID, it's our museum guy. Peter Wimper, 43, no arrest record. Uniforms are checking the whole yard but no sign of the missing crate. The Medical Examiner says someone moved the body. He wasn't killed here. The driver found him in the trunk of this stripped car a couple hours ago." Dean said.

"Time of death?"

"Nothing exact. Definitely within the last 24 hours."

"Shit."

"What? You know the guy?"

"No. I helped him change a flat tire last night. Around 8:30. He was a random guy on the side of the road. I never gave him a second thought."

"Well, that narrows down the time of death."

***

Adler approaches the ER entrance. He checks the time. He guesses he walked for over an hour. Exhaustion makes his body numb. The doors slide open and his mind begins working. He surveys the room like he's working a case. A man sleeps on the chairs to the right of the door. He's in his sixties and African-American. He wears dirty and torn clothes. He's missing one shoe. The sterile air fills his nostrils. The fluorescent lighting stings his eyes. His shoes clunk on the tile floor. Across the room, a younger couple speaks to a uniform police officer. The couple are the same height. They stand between five feet and five feet two inches, covered with tattoos and piercings. The female has a couple bandages on one arm. She has brown hair in a tight ponytail, wearing athletic clothes and flip-flops. The male has his left arm in a sling, shaved head, wearing a white tank-top and shorts two sizes too big with flip-flops.

"...and the dude pushed me into a window, broke the glass, cut up my arm real bad. I don't know if he was on drugs or somethin." The male says.

The officer stands a foot taller than the couple. He handwrites in a small notebook. He wears a pressed and clean uniform, shiny belt, boots, and badge. He has an expression of practiced objection. He yawns.

"I'm so sorry. It's been a long night. What happened next?" The officer says.

Adler approaches the reception counter trying to ignore the couple's conversation. The receptionist types on the keyboard fast, causing the fat on her upper arm to shake. She wears a pink and white flowery shirt with her blond hair in a bun.

"Can I help you, Sir?" She says.

"Is he good?"

"Oh, that's Pete. He got PTSD in Vietnam. He comes in here trying to get pain killers. I tell him no every night then he sleeps a couple hours and leaves. He's harmless. What about you? What brings you here?"

"I woke up next to my car. I have amnesia, maybe a concussion. I don't know if I got mugged or fell."

"Okay. I'll need you to fill out these forms. Write as much as you can remember. When you finish that, we'll bring you back and check your vitals and stuff and then the doctor will check you out, okay?"

"Thank you."

"You're very welcome."

I hope I can remember my medical history. At least I know my name.

"Paging Doctor Mercedes. Doctor Mercedes to Oncology. Paging Doctor Mercedes. Doctor Mercedes to Oncology." The intercom says.

Mercedes. I know someone named Mercedes. Who do I know named Mercedes? I saw her tonight. Was it tonight? The blond in the maroon dress.

***

The phone ring startled Adler.

Goddamnit.

"This is John Adler, Private Investigator. How can I help you?"

"Hello Detective. I know about the case you're working. I know what happened at the warehouse."

"Who is this? Who did you bribe for the information?"

"No bribing. Peter Wimper told me. Meet me at Sheri's Diner in one hour. I'll be wearing a maroon dress."

Is it the same woman from Vero Italiano? If it is why didn't she try to talk to me then? Sheri's has the best pie in town. Even if she's a reporter, I'll still get pie.

Adler arrived fifteen minutes early and waited in his car across the street. He watched the diner like a beast stalking its prey. The cook was short. Adler only saw his hat bouncing back and forth in the kitchen. The server refilled coffee and checked on everyone in the diner. An older couple sat in a corner booth. One man in a suit sat on a bar stool reading a newspaper. A family of four sat in a booth on the other side of the diner. He didn't see his mystery caller until five minutes passed.

A woman in a maroon dress and heels got out of a cab. She hurried into the diner looking over her shoulder several times. Adler exited his car and crossed the street while the woman chose a booth nearest the front door. The woman rubbed her hands together while the server poured coffee.

"Hi, Hun. Sit anywhere you like. Can I start you off with some coffee?"

"Yes, ma'am and I'd like a slice of that banana cream pie."

"Sure thing."

The server hurried off to get Adler's pie order. The woman held her coffee with both hands.

"Detective?" She said.

"And who might you be besides an associate of Mister Wimper's?"

"You could say we had an intimate relationship. I'm Mercedes Chase. I saw you at Vero Italiano earlier today."

"You did. Why didn't you speak to me then?"

"I didn't know who you were, and I hadn't heard about Petey. I didn't know he was…"

The server returned with Adler's pie and coffee along with a bell creamer.

"Can I get you folks anything else?"

"No, thank you." Adler said.

Mercedes poured creamer into her coffee.

"He called me last night. He told me about escaping the warehouse. He said everyone died, but he thought someone was still following him. He even told me about you helping him with his flat tire. That's why I called you and not the police."

She stared at her coffee, stirring it. Her left hand clutched the mug handle.

"What time was this phone call?"

"I'm not sure. Maybe close to 10 o'clock. I was in bed reading and didn't notice the time."

"Do you always read before bed?"

"Yes, except on weekends."

"What did he say exactly?"

"He told me he was in trouble and hurt. I asked him what he meant, and he said someone shot him but that he was okay. I asked him how he got shot and he said someone tried to steal a statue from him. I asked if it was from the museum. He said no that nothing was missing at the museum which I thought was strange. Why would he tell me nothing was

220

missing unless something was missing? I told him to go to the hospital, and he said they'd get the police involved so I told him to come to my place. He said he didn't wasn't me involved. Then he gave me your name and number. He said you would have the statue and to call you if something happened to him, so here we are."

A bite of pie rested on the fork floating in midair as Adler stared at Mercedes.

"And you took almost 24 hours to come up with that lame ass story?" Adler said.

"What? That's the truth."

"No, it isn't."

"Yes, it is."

"Okay, well, when you're ready to talk, call me again. We can both have pie. Tell the server to keep the change."

"Wait. I may have left out some details."

"More like all the details."

"Okay. I gave him the idea to use the museum's account to buy valuable art, so he could sell it. Some rich guy always donated the money and Petey managed the inventory, so no one would notice. He went to sell it to a fence a couple days ago. I hadn't heard from him, so I called him last night. He said one guy got paranoid after looking at the statue and thought Petey was wearing a wire. Everyone shot everyone and Petey hid behind a car. When it was all over, he took the statue and left. He said someone was looking for him about the statue, so he was lying low and put the statue in a safe place. He gave me your name and number and said you'd help me find the statue. I asked him if you were a friend of his and he said you were some random guy he met."

"Then why give me the fake story?"

"If he told you where the statue was, you would already have it, but I can tell you don't. What did he tell you?"

"I helped him change a tire. That was it. I didn't even notice his injured arm. He said he had an old football injury and needed a jack. I don't know anything about a statue."

"Well, I know a couple places he might have put it. Would you be willing to help me look?"

"I am a private investigator. My daily rate is two hundred dollars."

"I'll give you thirty bucks to help me for an hour."

"Deal. Where are we going?"

"It's a house on Burgess Street. Petey inherited it from his uncle. He uses it for storage. That's the first place we'll look. It's not far from here."

"Where's the place?" Adler said.

"It's a couple miles away, I think. I've only been there one time." Mercedes said.

Adler drove in the direction Mercedes' cab had come from. They sat in silence. Mercedes continued rubbing her hands.

"You seem anxious."

"Turn left at the next street."

"Did you know what statue Wimper was going to sell?"

"He said it was a cat statue with jewels or something. He said it had some kind of curse. I'm starting to believe him. Turn right."

"Are we close?"

"Yes, it's that dark house on the right."

Adler parked on the street.

"Do you mind if I keep my purse in your trunk while we look around?"

"Sure. No problem."

Adler opened his trunk with his keys. He turned. Mercedes had gone. Something hit him on the head, and he fell next to his car.

3

Adler wakes on a hospital bed. A nurse writes on a clipboard next to him. He pays no attention to her features.

"Oh, hello. How are you feeling?"

"Like someone smashed my whole body with a hammer. Is it after midnight yet?"

"Half passed. Is your memory coming back?"

"Some minor things are foggy like what I had for lunch, but the important stuff is clear."

"Good. I'll have the doctor come in to give you one last look and if he gives the okay, we'll send you home."

"Thank you."

He runs through everything he can remember. He focuses on the moments before getting knocked out.

Mercedes hit me. But why? I didn't have the statue. Searching the house was an excuse to get me somewhere alone. I should call Dean and have him check it out. What's the woman's role in all this? She knows more than she admitted. I can't get emotional. I need to stay impartial.

Adler hears the commotion in the ER. He doesn't expect to see the doctor anytime soon.

After two hours and an MRI scan, the doctors released Adler and told him to get rest and relax for a couple days. He took a cab home making a note to call Dean in the morning and pick up his car. He didn't plan to follow the Doctor's orders, but he would sleep for eight hours before driving.

He returned home to hear sounds of pain coming from his cat. The sound was a strange cross between a moan and an old police siren.

"Mmmwooe!"

"What are you upset for? You have food and water."

"Mmmwooe!"

223

"Are you upset because I wasn't here to pay attention to you?"

"Mmmwooe!"

"Well, you're gonna hate me more because I'm going to sleep."

The cat purred as Adler help her on his right shoulder like someone would burb a baby. He fell asleep with his cat kneading and purring on his stomach.

The phone rang and startled Adler awake. The sunlight felt brighter than normal and his head pounded harder than the night before.

"This is Adler."

"John, we got an update on Wimper. The ME says the time of death was between midnight and two am. They dumped the body sometime after that. We found an empty shipping crate at his place, but someone ransacked that too." Dean said.

Adler fumbled around looking at pill bottles until he found aspirin.

"What time is it?"

"A little past 10. You have a rough night?"

"I'll explain when I see you. Can you run a search on someone? A woman named Mercedes Chase. She's involved in the robbery, but I don't know how much she knows. I'm gonna shower then meet you at the station and give you the details."

"How did you get her name?"

"She called me last night. I'll explain later."

"I'll see what I can dig up on her. Take your time. I don't plan on going anywhere before lunch."

Adler felt groggy and foggy on his way to the police station. He took a cab.

"Jeez. You look like Hell." Dean said.

"That's the sweetest thing you've ever said."

224

"You meet up with that Chase woman. She give you a run for your money? She spend the night with you?"

"I haven't had coffee yet. I will punch you."

"Hey, Stevens? Can you get the Detective here a coffee? Thanks. So, what happened?"

"I spent the night at the ER. Got a blow to the head, had a concussion, and I'm not sure but I'd bet it was Chase."

"You talk to her?"

"She called me last night, said she knew Wimper. I met her at a diner. I don't believe anything she said except that fencing the statue was her idea."

"She tell you about it?"

"Yeah, some cat statue with jewels. Worth a couple million. Anyway, she says she thinks Wimper hid it at a place he owned. We drove over, I got knocked out, woke up with amnesia. My car is still there. I suspect the house is bogus, but I want to check it out. You got anything?"

Stevens brought Adler a coffee and left some files on Dean's desk.

"Thanks. So, Mercedes Chase got brought in a couple times, but never arrested. Guess who's her cousin? Jesse Bulger."

"Shit. That's not enough to get a warrant. Can you get some guys to bring her in?"

"She said she was in it with Wimper?"

"Yeah. Said it was her idea."

"The judge will sign her warrant. Let's get your car while we wait. We can get lunch on the way."

"You've been talking about food a lot more."

"Jeannie wants me to go on a diet. She keeps buying healthy food, and it's not filling. I've been losing sleep because I'm so damn hungry."

"I don't envy your life."

225

"Do you have anyone in your life? Or is it all cases and coffee?"

"My cat is the only woman I need in my life."

"Huh. I always thought you liked guys."

"Never had much interest in anyone of any gender."

"Unless they're a dead body. Where you wanna get lunch?"

"Someplace that has better coffee than the police department."

"Everywhere has better coffee. They get the cheapest shit."

"Better than Army coffee."

"You learn that after one year of ROTC in college? Whatever happened with that?"

"Didn't stick. Military officers are uptight. At least the ones I met were."

They picked up a quick lunch then found Adler's car where he left it. After checking everything was intact, Adler and Dean approached the house.

"This place is empty. You think it's Wimper's?" Dean said.

"No. Chase picked a random house to get me alone. She may not have known it was empty."

"We'll find out who owns it. This where you woke up?"

"Yeah. Trunk was open, keys under the car, Chase was gone. I was out anywhere between 20 minutes to an hour."

"Anything missing from your car?"

"I don't remember. I had the paper in my back seat, usual stuff in the glove box and trunk."

"Let's check the trunk. Maybe she took your tire iron."

Adler opened the trunk. There was a tire iron, jack, red rags with black stains, and a small toolbox.

"Everything there?" Dean said.

"I think so. It's foggy, but I thought I had a bag or something over here. Shit!"

"What? She took something?"

"When I helped Wimper change his tire. I was under his car working the jack. I bet he put something in my trunk and told Chase to get it. That's why she kept giving me those bullshit stories. Forget the house. We need to find her now before she ends up dead."

"I gotta update my Captain, I'll have her put out a BOLO."

"Your Captain?"

"Yeah. She says her wife knows someone at the museum. She'd take over the investigation if she could."

"When she tell you this?"

"This morning before I talked to you. There a problem?"

"No. Still got a headache. I'm gonna check the diner I went to last night then pay Bulger another visit."

"I'll get every uniform I can to look for Chase. I'll check back with you by the end of the day."

"Okay. Don't work too hard."

"I got you to do the work for me."

Adler thought for a moment before driving back to the diner. Recalling the directions from Mercedes. He recognized none of the staff. He checked his receipt to find his server's name.

"Excuse me. Was Lisa working last night?"

"Yeah. She works tonight too. She comes in soon. Oh, she's pulling in right now."

"Thank you."

Adler met Lisa at the door.

"Excuse me. John Adler. You're Lisa?"

"Yes."

"Do you remember I came in last night and sat with a woman? Maroon dress?"

"Yes. You ordered coffee and pie."

"Right. After we left, did she come back any time last night?"

"No. Is she in some trouble?"

"No ma'am. She's a family friend and going through a hard time. No one's seen or heard from her since last night and I want to check on her."

"She looked worried about something. She comes here a lot though. He name's Mercedes, right?"

"Yes."

"Yeah, I remember cause of the car name. If I see her, I can let her know you're looking for her."

"Here's my card. Call me if you see her. You don't have to tell her anything. I don't want her to worry. I want to know she's okay."

"Sure thing. No problem. Oh, you're a private detective. Oh no! Her boyfriend's cheating on her."

"Why do you say that?"

"She hire you to follow him? He doesn't treat her right. She's always telling me and Gail how awful he is. She won't say anything because he threatened to tell her cousin or brother or something. I guess they're business rivals and she doesn't want to cause family drama."

"Did she ever tell you his name?"

"Ray. Never heard a last name. I hope you catch that bastard in the act. She deserves better."

"I'll do my best. Thank you for your help."

"Come back and see us. Tell us what happened."

"Okay. Bye."

Adler returned to Bulger's office building and saw the same receptionist, Meghan.

"Mister Bulger is very busy. I can get Mister Willis to come speak to you."

"I'll speak with both of them. Tell them this is about Mister Bulger's cousin, Mercedes Chase."

Meghan whispered into the receiver not realizing Adler could hear her.

"Mister Willis. It's the detective again. No, he wants to speak to both of you. Yes, Sir, I know, but he says it's about Miss Chase. Yes, Sir. Yes, Sir, I will. Mister Willis will see you in his office. Take the elevator to the top floor. Take a left down the hall. It's the third door on your right."

"Thank you, Meghan."

Adler followed the directions arriving at Mister Willis's office. The door sat open with Willis sitting at his desk typing.

"Detective. Please come sit down. Mister Bulger will join us shortly and I am finishing. This. Email. So, what's this about with Miss Chase? I thought you were looking into some murders on one of our properties."

"I still am, and Miss Chase is a suspect. I'd like to wait for Mister Bulger before saying anything more."

"I understand, but you don't think she killed those people, do you?"

"Not directly, but she admitted involvement with the person who did. Where is Mister Bulger?"

"Right here." Bulger said.

Adler turned to see Jesse Bulger standing in the door. He wore an expensive gray suit, brown leather shoes, brown tie, and a white shirt. He stood as tall as Adler with graying, thinning hair and a thick salt and pepper mustache. He was broad shouldered and stocky. Adler considered Bulger to look like an older version of himself.

229

"What kind of trouble is Mercedes in now?" Bulger said.

"Theft, murder, assault."

"Little Mercedes? The worst she's done is break a man's heart. The hearts of many men."

"Rumor has it she's dating Ray Gallow."

"What?"

Bulger's tone changed. He walked next to Adler.

"What's he doing with her?" He said.

"Something to do with a statue. But you know all about that."

"Mister Bulger, it would be wise for you to consult with your lawyer before…"

"Quiet Willis. How much do you know Detective?"

"Enough. My concern is finding Chase before someone kills her. Everyone else involved is dead as far as I know."

"You plan to arrest her?"

"I'm a private investigator not the police, though I have reason to press charges. She knocked me on the head last night and gave me a concussion."

"What if I hire you to find her and pay you extra to cover your medical bills?"

"Sure, but you can't hold back. Tell me what's going on or I can't help her. Tell me everything about the warehouse, the statue, and the museum. I can keep her away from the law if I know what she's up against."

"You work for me now, so we got that client confidentiality or whatever, right?"

"Sure."

"Sir, I don't think we can trust…"

"Quiet Willis. The heist was my idea. I fronted the money to the museum and insurance would return my money if items went missing. It sounded simple and no one would get hurt. I had Mercedes get close to the museum guy to work something out. I don't know when she started seeing Gallow. She may have involved him from the beginning, I don't know. There was only one piece I wanted. It's a cat statue with sapphires all over. It's supposed to be worth a couple million. That's not why I wanted it.

"The rumor is it's cursed. I don't know if that's true, but it's never supposed to leave it's resting place in Madagascar. We never confirmed how many people died trying to get it back to the States. What those locals call cursed; I call greedy men. I'm one of those greedy men. There is a nice little folk tale that goes with the story, but I don't get how that makes something cursed. You can figure that out too.

"Natives call the story the Cat and the Rat. They both wanted to cross a river, but it was wide, and the current was fast. The Rat could swim but both animals worried about crocodiles. They decided to make a canoe out of a potato."

"A potato?" Adler said.

"It gets better. They eat part of the potato to make a canoe. The Rat paddled and got tired and hungry. The Cat was also hungry. The Rat decided to eat a part of the canoe and the Cat told him not to eat too much so they don't drown. The Rat promised not to eat anymore but did anyway. The canoe started filling with water. The Rat jumped out and swam to shore dodging crocodiles. I fucking hate rats. When he was safe, he laughed at the Cat. The Cat got so angry, she struggled to shore and pounced on the Rat. The Rat cried and begged, but the Cat said don't bother me and ate the Rat. A common saying in Madagascar is 'Don't bother me, said the Cat.' How's that story make something cursed?"

"I don't know. Maybe the curse only affects people who act like rats." Adler said.

Bulger and Willis laughed big, hearty laughs.

231

"I like you Detective. So, what's your plan?" Bulger said.

"Find Chase and figure out how Gallow fits. The bodies at your warehouse?"

"Not ours. Chase was gonna bring me the statue. I guess she and the museum guy wanted to sell it for themselves. I admit to the heist, but I didn't have anybody killed."

"Okay, I'll see what I can dig up. Call me if you hear from Chase."

"Willis, walk the Detective out. Give him your full cooperation."

"Yes, Sir."

"One more thing before I go. You know anything about the museum break in?" Adler said.

"I only know what I read in the paper." Bulger said.

"Thank you for your time."

Adler and Willis returned to the lobby in silence.

"We appreciate your help, Detective."

"I'll call you when I have something."

4

Adler went home to wait for the call from Detective Dean. It was after 4 p.m. He sat on his couch with feet resting on his coffee table, his cat sleeping in his lap. The cat's purring grew louder.

"I should have named you buzz saw with a purr like that."

He stopped petting.

"Meow."

"I'm sorry. I should have known how many pets you wanted."

The cat sat up and kneaded on Adler's lap. He continued petting as she continued purring. The phone rang.

"This is Adler."

"It's Dean. We tracked down Miss Chase's apartment. It doesn't look like she's been there in a while, packages stacked in front of the door. The neighbor couldn't remember where the Super was so we're waiting on a warrant to check her place. Anything on your end?"

"Bulger hired me to find Chase before you."

"You still gonna help me out?"

"Nothing says I can't get paid twice for the same job. Rumor is she's been seeing Ray Gallow. Haven't gone to see him yet."

"I guess all the guys are chasing her."

"Hilarious. I'll go talk to him after dinner. You're welcome to tag along."

"I better not. Jeannie likes having me home at night. Stop by the apartment in the morning."

"Real quick. What's Chase's address?"

"Stonybrook Apartments on Jefferson Road. Apartment 47. The Super should get back in town in the morning."

"Okay. See you tomorrow."

Meow.

"What? You've got water and food, I'm petting you. What are you whining for?"

Adler visited Mercedes Chase's apartment before going to Ray Gallow's home. He picked the lock and stepped over the boxes in front of the door. He searched the apartment wearing vinyl gloves. He didn't find the statue or any plans on the heist or murders. He covered his nose as he passed through the kitchen. He left making sure not to disturb anything and avoiding the boxes at the door.

The drive to Ray Gallow's house was short. The house was not extravagant but much nicer than anywhere Adler had lived. Street lights illuminated as he approached the front door. He heard shouting inside. He peered through a front window to see Mercedes Chase tied to a chair and three men standing around her. He moved towards the front door. It sat unlocked and he crept in. He snuck into the kitchen and phoned the police leaving the receiver off.

"Where'd that slimy rat hide it? I know he told you."

"He didn't tell me, I swear." Mercedes said.

"Don't lie to me!"

"If I had it, I'd have sold it already."

"You're waiting for things to cool off before you get it. So, where is it?"

Adler peaked around the doorway. Mercedes noticed him.

"He has it!" She said.

"Shit."

"Get him!"

Adler ran out the back door around the house. Two of the men chased him. He ran out to the street ignoring his car. He hopped a wall to the house next door.

"Where the fuck did he go?"

Police sirens whispered in the distance.

"Tell the boss pigs are comin. That fuck must have called 'em."

Adler waited a moment. The sirens grew louder. He looked over the wall. A car pulled out of the driveway and sped off. Alder went back to the house. The men were gone. They left Mercedes tied to the chair; her face swollen and bruised.

"I'm sorry for sending them after you."

"It's okay. The police are on the way. You have the statue, don't you?"

234

"I did. I hid it in the house where I knocked you out. Sorry about that too. When I went back today, it was gone. Someone took it. I don't know who. No one else knew about it."

"Why did you hit me?"

"I realized you didn't know Petey put the statue in your trunk. I didn't want to risk you seeing me hide it. I'll tell you whatever you want if you keep me safe."

"We'll get you to a hospital and have a couple officers keep an eye on you."

"Jesse won't be happy about this."

"He hired me to find you and keep you safe."

"What? You talked to him?"

"Yes, and I know all about his plan. What I don't know is Gallow's involvement."

"I thought I loved him. I'm not sure of anything anymore. He wanted leverage over Jesse. Once he learned the value of the statue, he got greedy. I knew he was the violent type, but I fell for him anyway."

"Don't worry about that now. When the officers get here, ask to speak to Detective Dean. He's a friend of mine. Tell him everything you told me. I'm gonna' find that statue."

Adler slipped out the back door as officers came in the front. He left before more police arrived.

He drove back to the abandoned house. The handle on the back door laid in pieces, and he pushed it open. The house was empty and in disrepair. He checked cabinets and closets. He searched for holes in the walls and loose floorboards. He looked in the crawl space in the ceiling. There was no evidence of a statue or anyone coming or going.

"Is she playing me again? The back door wasn't broken this morning. She could've broken it. What's missing from this cluster fuck?"

Someone called to him as Adler returned to his car.

"This house sure is popular today."

"Excuse me?"

"I'm sorry, I live next door. Did something happen?"

"Who else was here?"

The neighbor was an older woman walking her Maltese dog. She wore a white blouse and light blue pants and sandals.

"You and that other fella were here this morning. Then the police were here and left. Later this afternoon a woman came by then left in a hurry. She looked upset."

"The house is empty. The man you saw me with is a police detective. I'm sure he sent the officers out."

"What about that woman?"

"The home owner I suspect. Someone got in through the back door. Probably some teenagers having fun."

"Oh, my! I'll notify our neighborhood watch."

"That's a good idea ma'am. Keep your neighbors informed."

"Oh, I will. Thank you. Say goodbye Sweetums."

The Maltese had no interest in Adler.

Adler returned to the police station the next morning and found Dean with his Captain.

"So, what's the story with Chase? She take the statue or not?" The Captain said.

"Yes ma'am, but someone took it from her. The empty house we were at yesterday morning was empty. A neighbor said a couple officers were there after us and before Mercedes came back for the statue." Adler said.

"I didn't send any guys there. You suspected it was a distraction." Dean said.

236

"I was wrong. They were someone's hired goons dressed like police."

"Or we got crooked cops in my precinct. This stays between us. You understand, Detective?"

"Yes, ma'am."

"As far as anyone knows, your case has nothing to do with our stakeout tonight."

"What stakeout?" Adler said.

"Some crime bosses are meeting tonight. We're hoping to overhear what we need to arrest a few. We'll need all the hands we can get. You can tag along but you gotta' stay with Dean."

"Sure thing, Captain. I'm used to keeping him out of trouble."

"Tomorrow find out what else that woman knows. I got a feeling she hasn't said everything." The Captain said.

"She has a habit of that."

"Dean will get you the details of the operation tonight. Don't be late."

Adler and Dean walked back to Dean's desk.

"She gets straight to the point. You didn't even introduce us."

"Oh, I'm sorry. Detective Adler this is Captain Salazar, the woman who's been busting my balls for three years. She's not a fan of small talk."

"Is that it or is she not a fan of you?"

"Come on, everyone loves me."

"I don't."

"You're an ass."

"You're just now figuring that out?"

"Shut up. Here's the address. Go home and get some rest. Meet us there at 9pm."

Adler arrived at the address with minutes to spare. He met with Detective Dean and Captain Salazar.

"SWAT will take point followed by uniforms. We'll mop up whatever's left. It should be quick and clean with few casualties." Captain Salazar said.

"We can't move until they make the exchange." Dean said.

"Keep an eye on them. I gotta make a call."

"Who's she calling this late?" Adler said.

"Her wife. I already talked to Jeannie. She always leaves me extra food in the oven on these late nights. It doesn't matter what time it is or how tired I am, I'm always hungry when I get home."

"I have a similar problem except it's my cat that's always hungry when I get home."

"You need someone in your life besides that cat."

"You mean like a dog? I already got you."

"I mean another human besides me, smartass."

"You're irreplaceable, Dean."

"Stop it, I'm getting misty."

"Now who's the smart ass?"

"What's so funny?" Captain Salazar said.

"Nothing Cap. Old friends giving each other shit."

"Well, keep it down. We need to hear when it's time to move in."

"Yes, Captain."

"She does bust your balls." Adler said.

"What was that, Detective?"

"I told Dean here he needs to stop acting like a kid."

"I've been telling him that for years. Stay alert you two."

"Yes, Ma'am."

"Yes, Captain."

When they felt it was safe to, they both snickered under their breath.

"I'm so happy I work in the private sector."

238

"Any chance I could join you? I'll work at the office. I don't want to take pictures of husbands or wives."

"Sure. I could use a secretary."

"Don't be a dick. I'm serious. What do you think?"

"I'll consider it. But that's all."

"I guess that's better than nothing."

It was after ten when they got the green light to move in. The raid was over as soon as it started. With superior numbers, the police took control of the warehouse in a matter of minutes.

"One of these guys got away. Somebody must have tipped him. We have a mole." Captain Salazar said.

"Any ID on him?"

"Surveillance said someone called him Ray. That's all we know so far."

"Was it Ray Gallow?" Adler said.

"I don't know. Can you ID him?"

"Yes."

"Let's check the tape. Swanson! Roll the tape back to the guy who split."

"Yes, Captain."

"Is that him?"

"That's definitely Gallow."

"He didn't say or do anything on tape. At least not enough for us to hold him. I wouldn't worry about him." Captain Salazar said.

"He's involved with Mercedes Chase. That's who was beating her." Adler said.

"That's not what she said in her report."

"She's afraid he'll kill her if she accuses him."

"She needs to confirm that statement before we can get a warrant for him."

"We'll check on her tomorrow." Dean said.

"Go now. I can get a warrant first thing in the morning."

"Yes, Captain."

"Hey, Dean? Why don't you go home to the wife? I can get her statement. Besides, she already knows me."

"And you're working for her cousin. Is there something I should know?"

"You know as much as I do, but she might say more if she thinks I'm there for her cousin and not the police."

"Good point. You think there's more to this?"

"The police at Chase's house and Gallow getting tipped off make this more complicated."

"Yeah. Get something out of her. Half of what she says is never honest."

"I could say the same about you."

Adler did not need much persuasion to get passed the nurse.

"Fifty bucks."

"No problem. Has she had any visitors today?" Adler said.

"Not since I've been here. I haven't done my rounds yet. You mind if I check her out while you're in there?"

"Go ahead. I have a few questions for her."

"She's probably asleep this late. I still gotta check on her. Wait a minute."

The nurse hustled into the room. All the monitors were off. She checked Mercedes' pulse.

"She's dead. I'm sorry, Sir. I need to call this in. You need to leave. Here's your money."

"Keep it. I need to check your visitor logs. Contact the police after you call it in. Someone killed her."

"The log is here on the desk."

"Okay, Bulger was here this afternoon. That's her cousin. And Peter Wimper? Was this before you got here?"

"Yeah, a couple hours before."

"Before the raid."

"What?"

"Nothing. I was never here."

"Okay, but..."

"Here's another fifty."

Adler drove to Gallow's house, still covered in police caution tape. Believing no one was there, he drove to the warehouse district. The warehouse with the bodies from a few days before also had police caution tape.

This is as good as any place to look for him. Someone must have posed as Wimper at the hospital. Someone pretending to be her boyfriend. Gallow. He has a motive.

Adler crept through the dark warehouse. If someone were there, he wanted to surprise them. Silence. He stopped a few times to focus his hearing. Sweat rolled down his face. His legs felt heavy. Saliva filled his mouth. His eyes adjusted to the darkness. A moving shadow caught his eye.

My mind's playing tricks on me. Nothing to feel alarmed about. I'm seeing things. I'm the only one here.

Adler moved forward. The silence fueled his fear.

Doesn't this place have rats or spiders? I should hear something. The wind even.

He stopped. Listening.

That was two taps like shoes on the concrete. I'm certain. Someone's behind me.

He clenched his fists. He took a slow, deep breath and exhaled. His face felt cold as the blood rushed to his arms and legs. He turned.

A blow to the head knocked him on the floor. He saw two legs in front of him and they faded into the darkness.

241

5

Adler struggled to open his eyes. His head throbbed. He sat in a chair, arms tied behind, legs tied to chair legs. The light hurt his eyes. He shook his head to clear his vision.

"Yo, he's waking up." A man said.

"Who's there? Where am I? What do you want?" Adler shook his head again. The lights hurt less.

"Wake up, sunshine."

"Gallow. You the one who clubbed me?"

"Sure did. I owed you one for invading my home. That didn't stop me from taking care of Bulger's cousin."

"Is that a murder confession? Did you use her to manipulate Bulger and Wimper? Or did you love her but couldn't have loose ends?"

"She's not the one I love, Detective."

Gallow turned around as Captain Salazar entered.

"Hey baby." Gallow said.

"Aren't you married to a woman?" Adler said.

"You ever met a bisexual before?" Salazar said.

"Well, yeah, but not a married one."

"He thought he had it all figured out." Gallow said.

"You probably need a little help ironing out the details now." Salazar said.

"I got it. You two plan the heist for the money but also wanna stick it to Bulger. You convince his cousin to set up the theft making Bulger think it's his plan. When the police get involved, you use your leverage as Captain to arrest Bulger and get the statue. You're the one who sent officers to search Chase's house and take the statue. How much did you pay those cops to keep quiet?"

"I didn't. He shot them. No one more silent than the dead. Their bodies are in the other room."

"Are you framing me for their deaths? That won't stick."

"No, you all die in a fire. I sent you in with two officers to look for the statue, but the thieves burned this place down."

"And you both walk away with the statue with no one looking your way. You know the statue's cursed, right?"

"I'm not superstitious. I'm surprised you are."

"I'm not but I believe in patterns. Everyone who's touched that thing is dead. I imagine you'll both be dead in a few hours."

"What? Are you gonna kill us?" Gallow said.

"Maybe you get hit by a car or shot by some punk. Everyone near that thing dies."

"He's so full of shit."

"Shut up, Ray. He's got a point. We can't take any chances."

"Are you actually falling for this?"

"Baby. Baby. It'll all be okay. This time tomorrow we'll be in another country."

"You two are cute together. I get it now. Your wife is ugly, and Mercedes was too needy for you." Adler said.

"They were a means to an end."

"So, this was all your master plan, not his?"

"I had this plan, and he had the means."

"Gallow, how do you know you're not a means to an end for her?"

"We love each other, asshole!"

"People always love money more."

"Don't listen to him, baby. He's trying to save his own ass." Salazar said.

"I'll get the bags." Gallow said.

"Now that it's just us girls, you're not planning to keep him around, are you?"

243

"Love has you jaded. You've never had it so you can't see when other people do."

"Yeah, okay."

Gallow returned with bags and the statue in his hands. He handed it to Salazar.

"So much trouble for this little thing." He said.

"The money we get will make all the trouble worth it. We could buy our own country with how much this thing is worth. Let's get out of here." Salazar said.

Left alone, Adler surveyed the room; an old office covered in papers, trash, and dirt. It had one door and no windows. He felt the zip tie around his wrists. He wrestled with it, trying to pull one hand free. The tie cut into and scratched his hand. He smelled the fire and saw smoke come under the door. He yanked one hand out from the zip tie without drawing blood. He stood to pull the chair legs out from the ties on his legs.

He walked to the door. He felt the heat from the other side. He hit the handle with the chair. It took three more hits before breaking. Smoke filled the room as the door opened. He covered his mouth and nose with his tie. The heat burned his eyes. The smoke blocked his vision. He moved slow watching for falling debris. He recognized the warehouse. He had never left. He saw the door he entered from across the warehouse. There was a clear path. He ran, coughing through the smoke.

He fell out the door into the cool, clear air. He coughed and gagged. He crawled to his car and leaned against it, breathing heavy. Catching his breath, he sat watching the smoke drift higher in the sky.

A gunshot echoed around the warehouses. Adler lifted himself up, got in his car, and drove towards the noise. Smoke and flames filled his rearview mirror. At the street's end, Gallow laid motionless, shot in the chest, staring up at Adler.

So much for love.

Salazar was gone. Alder heard sirens from fire rescue vehicles. He left.

How many people are in Salazar's pocket? Is anyone? Did she bribe those officers, or seduce them like Gallow? Is Dean mixed up in this? Why would he call me in if he was? He knows I'd never join a scheme like this. I guess I should assume the worst. He can still help even if he is part of the heist.

Adler drove to his office, muttering to himself about his friend's loyalties. He inspected the door before entering. He moved with caution. He examined the entire space. He sat at his desk leaving the lights off. He strummed his fingers on the arm of his chair.

How do I draw out Salazar? I can use myself as bait since she thinks I'm dead. I can have Dean put out a BOLO on me and make sure Salazar gets it. He'll do it whether he works for her or not. Where do I meet her? No chance near the warehouses. She'll never come. Sheri's Diner. They're still open. Salazar might not try to kill me there. Or she will. It's worth a shot. What do I say to Dean?

Adler sat thinking and kept strumming his fingers. He grabbed his phone and dialed.

"This is, um, Detective Dean."

"It's John. Sorry to call so late."

"John? What? It's almost 1am. What's going on?"

Adler heard a muffled voice behind Dean's.

"It's John. No, Adler. I don't know. I did ask him. Sweetie, I'll handle it. Go back to sleep."

"I'm sorry. I didn't mean to wake you both."

"It's all right, but if it's not an emergency, Jeannie will kill us both."

"Chase is dead. Murdered."

"Shit. What happened?"

"It was Gallow. I found him at the warehouse where the shooting happened. He knocked me out and tied me up."

"Are you still there? Where did you find a phone?"

"No, I escaped. They set the place on fire."

"They? Who? Gallow?"

"Gallow and Captain Salazar."

"Dammit, Adler. Are you drunk?"

"She planned this whole thing. She sent the officers to Chase's house to get the statue. She has it and Gallow's dead. His body is near the warehouse fire."

"I can see the smoke from here. What do we do?"

"Salazar is dirty. Are you?"

"How can you ask me that?"

"Are you? Answer the question."

"No, and I'm pissed you had to ask."

"Even if you were, I need you to tell Salazar I'm alive and where to find me."

"Why the Hell would I do that?"

"To set the trap. Tell her you have evidence I took the statue. You heard someone saw me at Sheri's Diner and you are going there with a few officers. Don't call her until after you get there. I'm the bait. You wait and catch her with the statue."

"What if she doesn't bring it?"

"I don't think she'll go anywhere without it. She needs me dead before she can cash it in."

"Are you sure about this?"

"If she's not involved, she won't care if you're arresting me. If she is, she'll want to arrest me herself. I'll meet you at the diner. Get a couple officers we can trust."

"I brought you in on this case to make my job easier not harder."

246

"You're welcome. See you soon."

Adler unbuttoned his shirt and walked towards a closet. He put on a bullet-proof vest and re-buttoned his shirt. He fidgeted with his shirt and vest before leaving.

Adler arrived at the diner and Dean waited for him.

"Salazar's on her way. Rumor is she used a burner phone along with her personal cell. She gave burners to two officers a couple days ago. Those two officers are missing." Dean said.

"Their bodies are in the burning warehouse. Everyone who touches that statue dies."

"You haven't died."

"I've never touched it."

"I thought Chase clubbed you in the head with the thing."

"I don't know what she hit me with. It doesn't matter. Don't touch the damn thing."

"She'll be here soon. What do you want to do?"

"I'll wait inside. Make sure she has the statue before moving in."

"Here. Take this radio. Keep the button pressed so we hear you, but you don't hear us."

"Is this how you wear a wire on a budget?"

"Something like that."

Adler entered the diner. The server was not one he had met before.

"Thank God."

"You say something, Hun?" The server said.

"Oh, no. Can I get a coffee and a slice of cherry pie?"

"Sure thing. Sit wherever you like."

Adler chose a booth centered in the diner. Everyone inside and outside the diner could see him. The clock on the wall read fifteen minutes before 2. Ten minutes passed before Salazar parked. She sat in her car for a minute. Adler sipped his coffee and took a bite while watching her from the corner of his eye. She carried a bag as she entered.

"Sit wherever you like." The server said.

Salazar approached Adler's booth.

"How did you get out?"

"When did you decide to kill Gallow?"

"You want a prize for being right?"

"Join me for coffee and we'll call it even."

"Police should be here soon."

"You turn yourself in?"

"Do I look that stupid?"

"You did bring incriminating evidence."

Salazar looked at her bag.

"You can't trust people these days."

"Agreed."

Adler took another bite.

"Did you tell Dean to call me?"

"He called? I thought that old man would be sleeping."

"You're a good liar. Too bad you don't carry a piece."

"You holding a firearm on me?"

"Under the table."

"That sounds like enough for probable cause."

"What?"

Police cars screeched to a halt behind Salazar's car.

"Shit! You did set me up."

Adler stood and grabbed for her pistol. They struggled. She kicked him in the groin. He fell to the floor. Dean and two officers ran inside.

"Captain! Lower your weapon!"

Salazar turned her pistol on the officers. Dean fired two shots in her torso. She dropped the pistol. She looked down at herself in surprise. She looked at Adler on the floor before falling. Blood trailed from her mouth. Her empty eyes stared at Adler.

Dean holstered his weapon as he and the officers walked over.

"You hurt?" Dean said.

"Only my pride. Woah! Don't touch it!"

An officer held the bag with the statue and had an awestruck expression.

"You still believe it's cursed?" Dean said.

"I have trust issues."

"What do we do with it?"

"Send it back home, I guess. We should box it up first."

"Can I go back to sleep first?"

"Don't you gotta write this up?"

"You ruined my night again. Next time I'm calling you at 1am."

"Forget next time. Let's retire. I don't want to be this sore again."

Adler slept most of the next day. He drifted towards the coffee pot. His cat sat on the counter with half interest in his movements. His phone rang.

"This is Adler."

"You sound awful." Dean said.

"Good morning to you too."

"It's the afternoon, but I'll take it. How are you?"

"Sore. Tired. I've had hangovers easier than this. Everything get handled?"

"Sort of. Your statement helped fill in most of the gaps. We had an issue a couple hours ago. We had an officer box up the statue for shipment. He died after a light post fell on him. A drunk driver ran into the thing last night, but it collapsed when this guy walked past. The FBI is looking into it and they confiscated the statue."

"How do you feel about the curse now?"

"I don't care. It's the Feds' problem. I owe you one for this. We all do. No one suspected the Captain."

"Don't mention it. I got lucky."

"Okay. So, when are you getting a cell phone? Or a watch?"

"Everyone's got a clock somewhere."

"It'd be easier to get ahold of you."

"You know why I don't have one."

"Yeah, I get it. But at least get a wristwatch. They still make those you know."

"I don't want something clunky on my arm."

"Then get a pocket watch, you old bastard. You can't stumble around half blind in the world because of one bad case."

"That was more than a bad case. You know that. I've got to get to the office."

"Yeah, okay. You need to talk about this stuff with someone."

"One day I will, but not today. I'll call you tomorrow."

"Okay. Bye."

Adler stood a moment then sipped his coffee. He scratched his cat's ear. She purred.

"That's why you're the only woman in my life."

Adler arrived at his office a few minutes before 3. He picked up the mail and newspaper from the floor. The headline on the front page read "Corrupt Captain Gunned Down." Without a glance he threw the mail on his desk. He threw his bullet-proof vest in the closet without hanging it. He sat at his desk and sighed. He stared at nothing until the phone rang.

"This is Adler."

"Hello, John."

"Bethany. What hole did you crawl out from?"

"I don't want to fight. How are you?"

"Surviving. You didn't call to make small talk. What do you want?"

"Your name is in the paper. I wanted to know if you were okay."

"Why the sudden interest?"

"I'm worried. Why are you being short with me?"

"You stop talking to me with no explanation then call me up months later acting like everything is fine. So, why the sudden interest?"

"I don't know. The paper said you escaped a fire and got kidnapped or something. I guess it stirred up some feelings."

"You can't walk back into my life without telling me what happened before. Why you left."

"I don't want to do it over the phone. Can we meet tonight?"

"I've got a case."

"What about tomorrow?"

"Depends on the case. It might take a while."

"Can we try next week? Please?"

"Yeah. I'll call you tomorrow."

"Okay. Are you sure you're okay?"

"I've been through worse. We'll talk tomorrow."

"Okay."

"Bye."

"Bye."

Adler massaged the bridge of his nose near the corners of his eyes. He sighed. He picked up a piece of mail then threw it back down and rubbed his face. His phone rang again. He scoffed.

"This is Adler."

"John Adler? The Detective?" A man said.

251

"Yes. Who is this?"

"My name is Paul Grisham. I have a problem. I read of your accounts in the paper. I'm not sure but my problem is something supernatural and you have experience in the area."

"I don't believe in the occult Mister Grisham."

"But you believe your eyes. You believe facts. I only ask that you look at the facts and help me solve the problem. Will you help me?"

"I charge two hundred per day plus expenses."

"Excellent. Meet me at the Natural History Museum this evening. There's a Gala so please dress for the occasion."

Adler set back in his chair.

Why do the crackpots always call me when I get my name in the paper?

About the Museum

The Morbid Museum began in 2015 founded by Siris Grim. It featured one exhibit titled "Killers, Monsters, and Madmen." Few saw this exhibit and there were rumors of closing. The curator focused more on featured content and made each piece something unique. Holding to the theme of death, each piece went through a vigorous selection. With more content, the museum created more exhibits. The museum's mission is to allow visitors to face their fears about death. The founder and curator wishes for everyone to view death as a friend. A friend waiting to help everyone's soul travel to their final resting place. The museum is always looking for new patrons and hopes to expand with more exhibits in the next few years.

About the Curator

There are few records about Siris Grim before 2015 when the Morbid Museum first opened its doors. Some have found his fascination with death unsettling. He speaks as though he has lived many lives. There is a wisdom behind his eyes hiding tragic experiences. He resembles his ancestors in old photos. This gives rise to conspiracy theories of immortality. When asked these questions, he replies, "Everyone will know the truth one day." Every morning, spectators observe him sipping coffee in his office. He always wears a black suit with black shirt and black tie. Ever the dapper gentleman.

"An understanding and acceptance of death offers one an appreciation for life." He says. He hopes many will learn valuable lessons from the exhibits in his museum. He offers no answers to questions about his education or prior work history. The man is an enigma wrapped in a conundrum. He looks amused by the persistence of questions. "You will know the truth one day. There are three things that never stay hidden for long. The sun, the moon, and the truth." He walks away with confidence in his reply. He greets the many visitors to his museum.

Siris Grim leaves one with more questions than answers. He looks amused with the mystery in which he shrouds himself. A patron once asked him if he feared death. He said life was the only thing that ever frightened him. A unique name. An obscure museum. A mysterious man. This is the basis of the world's intrigue with the Morbid Museum. It's not only the exhibits, but the curator behind them. It's part of the appeal. It's part of the branding. There's no better way to leave an audience wanting more than to never tell them anything. What lies behind the eyes of Siris Grim?

About the Author

James Pack has written several collections of poetry and short fiction, is a contributing writer for themighty.com and the Bipolar Writer Mental Health Blog. He manages his personal website as well as a local entertainment website for Tucson, AZ. He studied Theatre Arts at the University of Arizona and studied Entertainment Business at Full Sail University for his graduate degree. James is a board member and Treasurer for the Tucson Fringe Theatre Festival and works with many nonprofits and local artists in the performing arts community. He lives in Tucson, AZ. Visit his website to learn more about James. Thejamespack.com, @jamespackwriter.

James Pack wrote this bio in the third person and it makes him feel narcissistic and gross.

A Letter from the Author

I want to personally thank you for reading my collection of short stories. I hope you enjoyed it as much as I enjoyed writing. Some of these stories were written many years ago and I've gradually tweaked and edited them over time. A trained eye will notice which stories I've written more recently as they are better written.

I would like to formally ask that you tell your friends, colleagues, and acquaintances about my book and my other writing. Also, an honest review of the book is always appreciated. I will never ask for anything more than your honest opinion; good, bad, or indifferent. If you are not able to post a review to Amazon or Goodreads, you can always visit my website and send me an email.

Once again, thank you for reading my work and I hope you look forward to the next projects I release.

James Pack

Made in the USA
Middletown, DE
25 May 2021